A VAMPIRE QUEEN'S DIARY

BOOK 1 THE BEGINNING

BY

P A HARRELL

ACKNOWLEDGMENTS

I would like to thank my loving husband Randy "Camaz" for this wonderful life or death depending on how you look at it. He has been my anchor through the entire process. I would like to thank my best friend Louisa "Lisa" for standing by me while I was composing my diary. Lisa you are the best friend a vampire queen could ever ask for. I would also like to thank all of my family and friends who have stood by me through thick and thin making this book possible. I love you guys!

INTRODUCTION

Suddenly a man jumped from the roof of a building I was in front of and landed in front of me. I stopped dead in my tracks and looked at the man. He was very handsome with roguish features and burning crimson eyes. A shiver went down my spine, for this was no man. This was a vampire! He grabbed my arm and said, "Good evening little vampire, are you looking for me?" I looked at him and said, "Why would I be looking for you? You are a vampire!" "The smell, little one, the one you are tracking, that is me!" "That is impossible! Vampires do not have that smell, only humans do!" "Oh, that is were you are wrong, little one. If a human that has done very evil things is bitten and changed a small amount of that smell stays with them!" I tried to pull away from the man, but he was to strong!

Chapter 1

FIRST SIGHT

In the spring of 1974 I was on vacation in Mexico and had decided to go shopping at a local dress shop. My driver had dropped me off at the shop and was to pick me up around 9pm. As I waited on the street corner for my ride I was approached by a handsome Mayan man with a body that would stop traffic! He asks me if I was lost. I answered, "No sir, I am just waiting for my ride." The man then responded,"You know such a lovely lady should not be out at night alone. These are very dangerous times! Do you mind if I stay with you until your ride comes?" I thought for a moment. He seemed like a gentleman and didn't seem dangerous. I answered his question, "No, I don't mind. May I ask your name?" He gave me an odd look and responded, "My name is Camaz and I am pleased to meet you!" "Hi Camaz, my name is Anne and I am pleased to meet you as well!" He smiled at me and shook my hand. We stood talking for about 15 minutes when my driver arrived. As I began to say my goodbyes to my new friend he asks, "I will be here tomorrow to finalize a deal I have been working on. Would you like to have dinner with me?" I thought for a minute, I don't even know this person, but he seemed like an okay guy. Then I thought, remember your built in radar, it has never led you astray. As I thought about it a little longer I agreed. I had always been able to tell, for some reason, when I was in danger. I did not feel in danger with this man, so I agreed to meet him the next night. As I waited, in the lobby of the hotel I was staying, for Camaz to pick me up for our dinner date I went over everything in my head from our meeting yesterday. I liked this man and felt comfortable with him the whole time we were talking. I had not felt threatened in any way. So why was I so nervous now? But I could not dwell on that now. Camaz had just walked through the lobby doors and was headed my way. He smiled when he saw me and all of my

nervousness went away! What was it about this man! Both

times he was near me I felt completely at ease. He walked up

to me and said, "Well Miss Anne, are you ready to go?" I

smiled back and answered, "Yes Camaz. Where are we going

for dinner?" "I know of a very nice restaurant on the outskirts

of town that has the best seafood in town. I have made

reservations for us for 9pm. Are you ready to go?" Trying not

to seem to eager, I answer, "Yes, if you are." As he walked me

to his car I was thinking, "What is it about this guy?" It's like I

have known him my whole life and I hadn't even known him

for a day! As we drove out of town he asked me questions

about myself, "How long are you going to be in Mexico?"

"Only for a few more days, I will be going back to The States

on Friday." We talked for a little longer and then he asked, "If I

am not being too forward, may I ask how old you are?" "I will

be 20 next month." "What day?" "On the 11th." "How old are

you?" "I will be 29 in August." I got to thinking, that's not too bad, he is only 9 years older than I am. I had thought he was much older by the way he spoke. So well mannered and knowledgeable. As we pulled into the restaurant parking lot he looked at me and said, "I have made arrangements for us to have dinner out back so we can be alone". We walked into the restaurant and Camaz gave the hostess his name. The woman smiled at us and said, "We have your table ready. Right this way." She led us through the restaurant to an open area in the back with a few rows of linen covered tables. We were escorted to the last table in the back. The smell of the flowers and plants at the corner of the open area was intoxicating! The table was almost to the edge of the woods. As we were seated the hostess handed us the menus and said our waiter would be with us in a few minutes. As I looked over the menu, I looked across at Camaz. There was a little sparkle in his eyes. I had never really looked into his eyes until now, so I had never noticed the color. They were the color of emeralds. I had never

seen a Mexican with eyes that color. Everyone I had seen had

always had dark brown. As I looked into his eyes, he cocked

his head slightly to the side and asked "What are you thinking

about?" I looked down quickly at my hands embarrassed and

said, "I'm sorry to stare, but I have never seen eyes the color of

yours." He smiled and chuckled, "You are very observant

aren't you?" The waiter appeared and asked if we were ready

to order. Camaz smiled at me and said, "Ladies first." I had not

taken the time to look at the menu as I was to wrapped up in

his beautiful eyes, so I ordered the first thing I saw on the

menu. "I will have the T-bone steak, rare, with a tossed salad."

The waiter asked what vegetables I would like with my dinner.

I told him none. He turned to Camaz to take his order. Camaz

looked at the waiter and said "I will have the house special."

As the waiter walked away Camaz looked at me and said "You

like your meat rare? Doesn't the blood bother you?" I thought for a moment and said, "No, not really. I like to taste what I am eating." He smiled at me and said, "Interesting. While we are waiting on dinner, would you like to take a walk? The plants in this area are quite beautiful." I responded without thinking, "Sure." As he rose from his seat he held his hand out to me. I stood and placed my hand in his. At once I felt something was off. His hand was very cold, almost like ice. How odd in this country with such heat! I pulled my hand back for a moment and said, "You are so cold! How could you be so cold in this heat?" He smiled at me and said "I'm sorry I frightened you. I have a condition where my body temperature runs a little colder than most." "That's okay, it just took me a little by surprise." I placed my hand back into his. As we walked into the wooded area behind the restaurant he began pointing out the different plants and flowers. I was amazed at how much he knew about each one. We stopped at an area where there were hundreds of blood red flowers. I stared at them and wondered what they could be. They smelled delicious! I asked Camaz,

"What kind of flowers are these?" "They are called nightshade,

they only bloom at night. Beautiful, aren't they?" "Yes, I think

anything to do with the night is beautiful!" As Camaz stared

into my eyes he asks, "Anything to do with the night? You're

not afraid of the night?" "No, I love everything to do with the

night!" As I stared into his glorious emerald eyes he suddenly

asked "Would you like to live in the night forever?" What an

odd question! Why would he ask such a thing? I thought about

what he asked and then it clicked. The strange eye color and

the cold skin! I began to back away slowly. He smiled at me

and said, "I thought you loved everything to do with the night?

That you were not frightened of the night". I stopped for a

moment even though my mind was screaming to run for

my life. I had seen enough vampire movies to know what I was

facing, but I could not run. As far back as I could remember,

being a vampire was all I ever wanted to be. Now with it

staring me in the face, what was I afraid of? I answered his question. "I am not afraid of you, or what you are." He smiled at me and asked, "And just what do you think I am?" I squared my shoulders and answered "A vampire." "You are not afraid of me?" "No, if I were I would not be here. This may sound strange, but it is what I have wanted to be since I was a child." He gave me a strange look and said, "All you ever wanted was to be a monster? Do you realize what you are saying?" I thought for another moment and answered, "I know it sounds strange, but it's what I have always wanted! I want you to change me!" "Do you know what you are asking of me? I very much want you to be with me, that is why I chose you yesterday. But I will not change you just for me. Do you feel the same way about me?" "I feel like I have know you my whole life. I have never felt the way I feel about you. Oddly, I think we were meant for each other." "Are you sure this is what you want? Once it is done it can never be undone! Do you think you could take the life of another human to sustain yours? Never growing old, never seeing the light of day again, and never seeing your friends and family. Are you ready for that?" I did not hesitate in giving him my answer. "Yes!" He walked slowly toward me and said, "The process takes 2 days and is very painful. Your body will try to reject the transformation. You will scream for death the entire time. When you have changed, the thirst will be relentless. But I will be with you the entire time, so do not be afraid. I will teach you how to hunt only the humans who do not deserve to live. I do not take the blood of the innocent. I will take you to my place when the transformation begins." He took me in his arms and kissed me slowly. I had never felt this way before and my body ached for him! I wanted him more than anyone else on earth! As he broke our kiss he stared into my eyes with a longing I had never seen before and said, "Are you sure this is what you want?" Breathlessly I moaned "Yes." He kissed me again for a brief moment and slowly started kissing down my neck. My body burned with pleasure and then, with one very sharp pain. it started.

Chapter 2

THE BURNING

At first I thought I was dying but then the pain of the burning began. At that point I wished I was dead! My whole body was burning from the tips of my toes to the top of my head! I screamed and shrieked, begging someone to kill me. But no one was listening, or I thought no one was listening. I heard his soothing voice whispering to me, "I know you are in terrible pain but it will be over soon and you will hurt no more!" But how could he say that? The pain was increasing not decreasing!! I screamed at him, "Camaz! Please kill me I cannot stand this pain anymore!" He whispered in my ear, "Love, this is what you wanted. Soon the pain will be gone and you will open your eyes to a brand new world." "But how much longer must I endure this blistering fire? I do not think I can take much more!" "Soon, my love. You have been burning

for a little over 2 days. It will not be much longer, I promise!"
As I lay there burning, my head began to clear. I could hear and
smell things so more clearly. I could hear my heart beating
franticly. Suddenly the fire seemed to change, leaving my limbs
and attacking my heart with a burn ten times hotter than before.
My heart began to race even faster, as if it was trying to out run
the blaze engulfing it. Suddenly I began to feel a different burn,
dull at first, in my throat, then becoming a blaze. I became so
thirsty! With one last thud, my heart stopped. The pain was
completely gone except for the blazing fire in my throat. I lie
very still for a moment and then open my eyes. As I looked up I
could see Camaz smiling at me. I thought to myself, "My god,
this is the most beautiful man I have every seen! I smiled back
at him and spoke for the first time. "Is it over?" "Yes, how do
you feel?" "Parched, why am I so thirsty?" "You are newly
born. The thirst is very powerful in the beginning. You must
now hunt or the pain will become unbearable." "Hunt! I don't

know what to do!" "I will teach you. Love, it is very easy to learn. But you must learn to kill only the ones deserving to die. You will be able to smell the evil in their blood. It has a very distinct smell. You must never spill the blood of the innocent." I started to stand and before I could blink, I was up. How strange, I felt like I was floating! "Why do I feel so light? How did I move so fast?" "You are Vampire, you no longer have the heaviness of a human's body. All of your senses are enhanced. You have strength, speed and a highly keen sense of smell now." "Why do I feel like I can fly?" "Because you will, once you have mastered all of your new abilities." "Are you kidding me?" I will be able to fly? "Yes Love, it will come to you soon." Camaz took my hand and pulled gently, "Come and sample all the night has to offer." We left the safety of our hiding place and into the night we went, in search of my first meal. We went into the heart of the city. Camaz explained what I was to look for in a human and what smell I was to be searching in the air. "It is a very distinct smell, under the very sweet, salty and metallic smell of blood is the smell of pure evil. You will only be able to smell it in very bad and wicked humans. You will know the smell when it hits you." I closed my eyes and let my sense of smell take over. Slowly I began to crouch and move forward. "Camaz, I smell something strange, but not in a bad way. It is almost like it is calling to me!" "Yes, that is what you need to sense. It is below the smell of the sweet blood. Just let it carry you until you reach your target!" Slowly, I started to pick up the pace. The wonderful smell called to me. My throat was suddenly on fire and all I could think of was quenching that thirst! I notice a man in the distance, just standing on the street corner. He looked very menacing. I straightened out of my crouch and began slowly walking up to him. As I walked past him I give him a timid smile and quickened my pace hoping he would pursue me. As I turned the corner, I heard his footsteps. I began to move a little quicker. He was right behind me. I stopped and acted like I was frozen in fear. He grabbed me from behind and placed his right hand over my mouth to keep me from screaming. There was an alleyway right beside us, so he dragged me into it. I struggled, but did not try to get away. The excitement of the hunt and the burning thirst had taken over completely. I broke his hold as if he were just a child trying to hold on to me. I slammed him into the wall, holding both his arms above his head with just one of my hands. I used my other hand to slam his head to the side. I stuck with the speed of a cobra, sinking my fangs into his throat. His sweet, warm blood flowed into my mouth and down my throat, quenching the burning thirst. As I drank, his struggles became less and less until he stopped fighting. I could hear his heart beating franticly, faster and faster. As I took his last drop, his heart gave one last thud and stopped. I released him and let him drop to the ground. I wiped my mouth on my arm and turned to see Camaz standing casually at the entrance to the alley. He said, "I must say, for your first time you have done quite well!" I looked at him lovingly and asked, "Why am I still thirsty?" "Because you are newly born, the thirst is very strong the first few years. It will lessen the older you become. If you would like, we can continue hunting." "Will you hunt with me this time?" He looked at me lovingly and answered, "Your wish is my command, Love!" So off we went, looking for my next meal. The following evening, when I awoke in Camaz's arms, I asked, "My love, what is on the agenda for tonight?" "Darling, I thought we would begin your training." "What kind of training? Do I need to learn more about the hunt?" "No, I thought I would give you your first flying lesson, that way you will have no need to have your prey pursue you." "Are you serious! You are really going to teach me to fly?" "Yes, my dear, most of it comes naturally, but there are a few things you will need to learn." A few hours later, we were standing in the middle of an open field deep in the woods. Camaz looked at me and said, "Okay, what I need you to do is watch what I do and then try it yourself." "Alright, let's get started!" I exclaimed with a nervous laugh. As I watched, Camaz crouched low and sprang straight up into the air, spread his arms and just hoovered in mid-air. He stayed airborne for about 3 or 4 minutes then floated slowly back to the ground. "See, Love, it is quite easy. All you have to do is spring up and think to yourself, "Do not fall, and you will stay airborne." "I don't know Camaz, I'm afraid I might fall!" "As I said before, my dear, it is quite instinctual. Just give it a try. I will catch you if you fall." I stood silently as I pondered the thought of actually being able to do what he had just done. If for some reason I did fall, I knew Camaz would catch me and even if he didn't, I was a vampire for crying out loud! I was already dead, it couldn't hurt to try! So I crouched low and sprang straight up into the air and I thought "Stop!" And I did, just suspended in mid-air! I did not fall to the ground as I had thought I would. Suddenly, I began to laugh with uncontrollable glee. Camaz shouted up to me, "Do you plan on staying up their all day, or are you coming back down here to me?" "Oh keep your socks on! I'm enjoying myself too much to come down just yet!" "You have much still to learn, my dear, and we do not have much nightfall left. Also, I'm hungry!" "Alright spoil sport, I coming!" Slowly I began to descend toward the ground, and landing right beside him and said, "Are you happy now? What's next on the agenda?" Staring deeply into my eyes he said, "We hunt!" He grabbed my hand and pulled me toward the edge of the woods. We ran, like the wind, back to the city and reached downtown in no time. He pointed up to the top of one of the buildings and I understood at once and leapt to the top of the building. He followed right behind me. We both landed on the roof at the same time. As we crouched on the edge, I closed my eyes and let my sense of smell take over. The smell of human blood was thick in the air and was very intoxicating! But I scanned further out smelling for the special scent that would tell me what I am looking for. Suddenly it was there. I turned to Camaz and said, "There, to the east, do you smell it?" "Yes" he replied. "There are two of them and they are hunting for their next victim. Looks like it will be a feast for the both of us!" I watched as the two men came into view. They were scanning the area, looking for an innocent woman. They were master rapists. They had raped and murdered many women. They reeked of it. I poised to strike, every muscle in my body tensed for the attack. They were right below us now. I looked at Camaz and smiled. We both dropped from the wall at the same time and landed on the rapists. My victim stared at me in disbelief. I caught his attention with my eyes and he went limp in my arms. I sank my fangs into the softness of his neck and began to feed. The sweet, salty blood flowed over my lips and down my throat, quenching my burning thirst. Camaz had the second man down on the ground and was slowly draining him dry. He looked up

from his prey and said, "They always taste better the more evil

they have done!" I looked at my victim and said, " Oh how

right you are!" "Have you had your fill for the night? Are you

ready to go home?" "Yes, I am ready to have your arms around

me and your lips upon mine!" I rolled off of Camaz, panting

wildly and said, "You know, one of these days you are going to

be the death of me!" "Silly dear, I already have!" I laughed out

loud and asked, "So, what will I be learning tomorrow night?"

"Tonight I taught you how to hoover. Tomorrow I will teach

you how to fly from one place to another. Also, I will be taking

you to our council for your formal introduction and permission

for us to marry!" "Camaz, you haven't even asked me yet!" I

snicker softly. "Then I shall do it now!" Camaz sprang from the

bed lifting me with him. He positioned me on the edge of the

bed and got down on one knee, looking up at me with those

burning emerald eyes and asked, "Anne, will you do me the

honor of becoming my bride?" He reached into the bedside

table and produced a small black velvet covered box and placed

it in my hands. I stared at the box, smiled and said, "Of course I

will marry you! You are my soul mate. I will love you forever!"

Camaz popped open the lid of the little black box. I looked

down at the most beautiful ring I had ever seen. The center

stone, a emerald cut two carat diamond was surrounded by

round blue diamonds. He said, "Anne, I promise to love you

until the end of time!" He pulled me to my feet, wrapped his

arms around me and kissed me passionately.

Chapter 3

INTRODUCTIONS

We awoke the following evening and rose from our bed. I looked at the ring sparkling on my finger and smiled. I still couldn't believe I was officially engaged! I turned to Camaz and said, " Alright darling, will we be practicing in the same field tonight?" "Yes, dear heart. Tonight you will learn how to fly, swoop down on your unsuspecting prey and carry them away." " I will be able to carry someone and fly at the same time?" "Yes darling, you are strong enough to carry ten men at one time!" "Are you kidding me? I did not know I was that strong!" "Yes and as you grow older, the stronger you will become!" Really?" I thought to myself, "Strong enough to carry ten men, how interesting!" I grabbed Camaz's hand and tugged lightly saying, "Okay, let's go, I am ready for flying!" We entered my training field and Camaz said, "Alright, I want you to watch me and learn." He proceeded to spring into the air then stop and hoover. He shouted down to me, "Okay, all you have to do from this point is spread your arms, bend and push off with your feet." He showed me how it was done and gently floated back down to my side and saying, "Your turn!" I smiled up at him and sprang into the air, stopped for a moment then spread my arms, bent and pushed off. To my surprise I was flying! I soared around as if I were a bird, laughing the entire time. Camaz shouted up to me, "Do you plan on coming down anytime soon, little bird of prey?" I laughed one more time and asked, "Oh, do I have to?" "Yes, we have places to go and people to meet before the night is over, and, I imagine, you are getting thirsty, aren't you?" I thought about that one, the burn in my throat was beginning to worsen, so reluctantly I descended back down to earth, thinking that I have eternity for flying! We headed deep into the Mexican mountainside. After traveling for a little while I asked, "Is it much further?" "No, just over the next hill." We reached the entrance of a cave and Camaz said, "The council resides in the underground caverns below." We began to descend into the cave. It was very dark but my eyes adjusted to the darkness and I was able to see just fine. We went down the pathway a little bit farther and entered a huge cavern. The area was like a small city. There were buildings everywhere. We walked up to a very impressive building, it looked like it could be a palace. I asked, "Do vampires have a king and queen? This looks like a palace!" Camaz laughed and said, "Yes my dear, we do have a king, but no queen as of right now." A very distinguish gentleman approached us and said, "Welcome back Sire. It has been a while! Who, may I ask, is this lovely lady?" I looked at Camaz and said, " Did he just call you Sire?" "Yes my dear, that he did. James, may I introduce you to your future queen, Anne." "My pleasure, Lady Anne. Sire, I must say you have wonderful taste!" "Thank you James! Is the council in court?" "Yes Sire, they are awaiting you." James bowed to me, turned and walked inside. I looked at Camaz in astonishment and asked,

"You were kidding about the queen thing, right?" Camaz smiled

at me and said, " To the contrary, my dear. I am the king and

you will be my queen!"As we entered the building I looked

around in astonishment! There was beautiful paintings on all of

the walls. The men and women in the paintings were very

handsome and beautiful, very regal in all of their pageantry! I

looked up at Camaz and asked, "Who are all of the people in the

paintings?" He looked at me and said, "Why, these are all of the

prior kings and queens of my kingdom." He took my hand and

led me to a painting of two men and a woman. As I looked at

the painting I noticed one of the men was Camaz and I said,

"Wow, Camaz is that you?" "Yes, my dear, and that is my father

and mother. They were the last rulers of our world. They were

killed by the humans many years ago and I became the king. I

have been searching for over 200 years for my queen, and now I

have her!" "Oh Camaz, I love you so much!" "As I love you my future queen!" We stole a quick kiss and then he proclaimed, "We must go see the council so our wedding plans and your crowning as my queen can be made!" We entered a huge hall with many people lined up on both sides. At the very far wall was a row of eight very beautiful chairs with four men and four women seated in them. They were adorned in very fine clothing and jewelery. We approached the council and Camaz spoke, "Good evening council. May I present Anne, my future bride and your future queen!" An elderly looking gentleman spoke up and said, "Welcome home, your highness, and welcome to our future queen, Anne! May I ask when the wedding planning is to commence?" Camaz said, "I would like the preparation to began immediately!" "Of course your highness, Lady Anne, I am Gabriel, head of the vampire counsel. On behalf of all of us, welcome! We look forward to you becoming our queen. It is so good to see King Camaz so happy. We have waited many years for this day!" He bowed to Camaz. We turned and Camaz led me back out into the city. As we were walking he looked into my eyes and said "They like you very much and approve of our union! Just tell me the day we are to marry and I will take care of everything." I looked into his beautiful eyes and said, "Is tomorrow too soon?" I giggled. He said to me, "I am sorry, my love, but it will take a few days for everything to be arranged. Do you think you can wait for me that long?" I giggled again and said, "My love, I could wait all of eternity for you!" "Then come let me show you the palace and introduce you to your ladies in waiting." I giggled again and we were off to the palace. We walked up a long and winding path until we reached his castle. It was the most beautiful place I had ever seen! We were underground but there were rose bushes everywhere. With blooms of every color imaginable and the smell, oh my god, the smell left me breathless! As we entered the castle there was a small group of women waiting inside. Camaz said, "Anne, this is Maria, Louisa, Carmen and Silvia. Your ladies in waiting.

Ladies this is your future queen, Anne." They all curtsied then a tall, thin and very delicate looking woman took my hand and said, "Hello, my name is Louisa, I am the king's sister." I said, "I am very pleased to met you Louisa and the rest of you ladies!" She pulled my hand and said, "Come, there is much to do." I looked at Camaz and he said, "Go my dear, I will catch up with you later and we will go hunting." I said okay as Louisa pulled me up a flight of stairs and into a large bedroom. "This will be your chambers, my lady, until after the wedding. Anything you need, all you have to do is ask. Now the first thing we need to do is begin working on the royal wedding gown. Maria is our seamstress and will be creating the gown to your specifications. Just let her know what you would like the gown to look like." So we all sat on the huge bed and I began explaining to Maria what I would like my gown to look like. I sketched a design I had always envisioned my dress to look like. And so my gown was born! Maria began work on it immediately. As I slipped into the beautiful dress Maria had

created for me and looked at myself in the mirror, for the first

time since becoming vampire. I was in total shock. Who was the

beautiful creature staring back at me? I was a pale, creamy

white with big beautiful deep blue eyes. My long brown hair

hung down my back in beautiful curls. Atop my head was the

diamond encrusted crown Camaz had sent to me the night

before. In the center of the crown was a blood red ruby. The

necklace and bracelets matched the crown to a tee! I still could

not believe this enchanting creature was me! If I could still

produce tears I would have cried! My ladies-in-waiting all

surrounded me and began congratulating me. There was a knock

on the door. A fine looking gentleman proclaimed, "It

is time my lady!" My girls, as I would call them later, began

filing out of the room one by one with me following. We went

down the long staircase, gracefully, and into the large hall where

the ceremony was to be preformed. There were hundreds of

vampires in attendance and they all stood and cheered as they saw me entering the room. As I walked slowly down the aisle, my eyes locked with Camaz's. He was dressed in a black tuxedo with a blood red rose in the lapel. God, I couldn't take my eyes off him! He was mine for all eternity and we would rule the vampire world together! Once I was beside him he took my hand in his and we turned to the head council leader and the ceremony began. We spoke our vows and swore to love and protect each other for all eternity, then we were proclaimed King and Queen by the council. I was later told the entire country had been searched for the most evil of all humans for our wedding banquet. What a feast it was! The two most evil of all were served to us. As I drank the blood of the man who had murdered many men, women and children I thought to myself, "One less evil doer in the world now!" After all the introductions and formalities were taken care of, we excused ourselves and went upstairs for our first night together as king and queen. Oh what a night it was!!!!

Chapter 4

QUEST TO SAVE ANOTHER KING AND QUEEN

One night, while we were out hunting, a very strange and unusual thing happened. A man approached us and stated he was from the council of American vampires and had come to ask us for a favor. "Sires, my name, is Jacob. I am the head council member of American vampires and our king and queen have been abducted. A great ransom has been demanded. The abductors have demanded that the king and queen of Mexico come to the United States and deliver the ransom. They have demanded twenty-five million dollars, to be delivered, by you in ten days or the king and queen will be destroyed!" We looked at each other and said, "You know this could be a trap just to capture us!" "Sires, we are well aware of the possibility and we will provide you with all the security needed, day and night! We have an army of werewolves that will protect you during the day and master warrior vampires to protect you at night."

Camaz looked at Jacob and asked, "If you have all of this

protection for us, why were your king and queen not

protected?!" Jacob replied, "We believe there is a traitor in our

high council. We believe he wants the king and queen destroyed

because he is next in line to take the throne! He has been put

under arrest, for the moment and has no contact with anyone.

He has been interrogated but has not given up the location of the

king and queen. All of the elders have agreed to the terms of

release and payment of the ransom, but we cannot proceed

without the two of you. Will you come to America and help us

secure the release of our king and queen?" Camaz looked at me

and said to Jacob, "We must discuss this with our council. We

will get back to you in a few hours. Please make yourself at

home in the castle. If there is anything you need, just ask the

staff." As we walked away I spoke to Camaz in a low voice,

"Do you think we will be as safe as he has said?" "I'm not sure about that, but we must go to the council first and discuss this. If they feel we should go through with the ransom delivery, I have some very special people for you to meet." At the meeting with the council, everyone was in agreement with us going. Camaz took my hand and said, "Come, my queen, I have some very special friends I would like you to meet." An hour later we arrived in the small town of Cristos and come to what looked like a military barracks. Camaz knocked on the huge door and a very well built Mexican answered the door. "Welcome Sire, we have been awaiting your arrival." "Stanos, this is my queen, Anne. Anne this is my right hand man, Stanos. He is in charge of the Vampire Elite Squad. They protect the king and queen." "Hello Stanos. I am very pleased to meet you!" "My Queen, the pleasure is all mine." He bowed, took my hand and kissed the back of it. Camaz said, "Stanos, are all of the squad here?" "Yes sire, and they are assembled in the war room awaiting your arrival." We walked down a long hall to a huge room filled with fierce looking vampires of many nationalities. There were also strange men that did not smell of vampire, but more of animal. I looked at Camaz and askd, "These men are not all vampire but they are not human either. What are they?" Camaz smiled down at me and said, "My war council consists of highly trained vampires, werewolves, demons and fairies." I looked at him and said, "Fairies, are you kidding me? They are cute little creatures that wouldn't hurt a fly!" There came a great roar of laughter from a group of men in one corner of the room. One of them approached us and Camaz said, "Anne, this is Dempie. He is a great fairy warrior and I would not consider him a cute little creature. Once you have seen him fight you wouldn't either!" Dempie walked up to me, bowed and then smiled, his mouth is full of razor sharp teeth! The handsome features I first saw disappeared in all those teeth! I asked, him, "Do you have wings?" He laughed and replied, "No, sorry only the females have wings." So we began going around the room and I was introduced to all of Camaz's closest and most trusted friends. When all the introductions were made and all the details of our trip were planned out, we returned to the castle. Talk about an interesting day! I got to meet all of Camaz's friends and found out that male fairies do not have wings! Our coffins were loaded into Camaz's private transport plane and we boarded for the flight to America. I was excited about returning to the US for it had been fifteen years since the wonderful night I met Camaz and I was a little homesick. Of course I could not see any of my family as they were told I died in a car crash many years ago. I wished I could go see them though, I missed my mother and father so much! But the life of a vampire must be kept secret for our protection! The large seats on board the plane were very comfortable and I relaxed reading a book I had picked up for the trip. A book about vampires, ha ha! We were still about eight hours from Washington state when daybreak came. So we retired to our coffins to sleep the sleep of death until our arrival.

I was shaken awake by the feel of the plane touching down. I looked at my watch and it was 9:45pm. I rose from my coffin and was greeted by my husband with a fiery kiss. I whispered into his mouth, "Where are we?" He pulled away and said, "We are in Seattle, Washington. We will be meeting with their council in about an hour, then we will be flying out to Atlanta, Georgia where the king and queen were abducted. They were at their summer palace when they were taken. Come, we must hurry, the council is waiting." We left the plane and headed into the heart of the city. About twenty minutes later we arrived at a very large home with towering pine trees on each side of the entryway. Camaz looked at me and said, "This is the home of Elder John Harrell. He will be updating us on all that has happened over the past few days." After getting the details of all that has happened we said our goodbyes to John and headed back to the airport. Our plane had been refueled and was ready for takeoff. The trip to Atlanta took about four hours, during which time I continued reading my book.

Chapter 5

SOUTHERN HOSPITALITY

We arrived in Atlanta at 9:20pm and we waited until all of our things were unloaded. We headed to the rental car lot where a large SUV had been reserved for us. Everything was loaded into the truck. We left the airport heading into the heart of Atlanta. Stantos, being from Atlanta drove us to our destination. We were going to the king and queen's home to meet their advisers. Camaz told me the king's head adviser was named Astor Stone and he has known him for many years. Camaz knew I was very worried about being in Atlanta and fearful of us also being abducted. He told me, "My dear, there is nothing to worry about we will be very well guarded!" I replied, "I know, honey, but I can't help it. This is a strange place and we do not know many of the people here!" We pulled into a long winding driveway and approached a large Victorian home surrounded by large trees. The home was stunning! A man was waiting at the door

when we pulled up. We all got out of the car and Camaz walked

up to the man and shook his hand then saying, "My good friend

Astor, it has been a few years! All is well with you I hope?"

Astor replied, "I am doing well, Sire, all things considered."

"Astor, I would like you to meet my queen, Anne." Astor looked

at me and smiled. He said to Camaz, "Well old friend, it is about

time you took a bride and settled down! My, such a beauty at

that!" Camaz smiled and said, "Yes, old friend, that she is!

Come let us go inside so we can discuss all that has happened."

We walked into the house and I just stared, opened mouthed, at

the furnishings! Everything was from a time long gone. A small

framed light skinned black woman approached us and said,

"Hello, my name is Jeannette, my lady, and I will be attending

to your needs while you are here. Would you like to go to your

room so you can freshen up after your long trip?" I answered,

"Yes, that would be very nice." Camaz looked at me and said,

"Yes, my dear, do go ahead. I will be up shortly. I need to speak with Astor for a while." We quickly kissed and I followed Jeannette up the stairs to our room. She opened the door for me and we walked in. The room was huge, a king size poster bed in the middle. Jeannette asked, "My lady, are you hungry?" I thought to myself, "Actually, the burn is getting a little strong" I said, "Yes, Jeannette, I am, but I do not know the best area to go hunting." She replied, "That is okay, we have the very finest of stock in the basement. Would you like a bath before your meal?" "Yes, that would be very nice." She pointed to the door on the right and said, "The bathroom is through there. While you are bathing I will put up your clothing". I responded, "Thank you Jeannette, you are very kind!" I went into the bathroom and closed the door behind me. While I relaxed and soaked in the tub, I thought, "Boy, talk about southern hospitality! I could get use to living in a place like this!" After about an hour I was bathed, dressed and ready for dinner.

Jeannette had unpacked all of Camaz and my things, she and I went back down stairs. We entered the library where Camaz and Astor were seated. Camaz looked my way, smiled and said, "You look beautiful as always, my dear! Are you ready for dinner?" I answered, "Yes, I am famished! The burn is almost unbearable!" "Then come and we will put out the fire!" We went to the lower basement of the huge house and there were many rows of cells, just like in a prison. Each cell held some of the human race's worst rapists and murders! Their sentence was nothing like they would have gotten in the human world! They were condemned to death at our hands. To us they were nothing more than blood bags for our next meal. I walked up to a cell and read the bio of the prisoner. He is wanted in ten states for many rapes and murders! He was responsible for the deaths of as many as seventy woman. I thought to myself, "Oh how sweet his blood is going to be!" I unlocked the door and entered the cell. The man was on a cot toward the back of the cell. He saw me approaching and I watched as he eyed me up and down. I spoke, "Do you know why you are here?" He looked at me strangely and said, "No, I just know I am going to get out of here one day and someone is going to pay dearly!" I laughed and said, "Oh, really? Well, bad boy, today is your lucky day! You will be getting out of here, but in a body bag!" I sprang on him and he tried to push me off but I just laughed. "It will do you no good to resist me! Now hold still, I am starving!" He looked into my face. I smiled at him, baring my fangs. He said, "What the hell are you?" "My dear, I am your worst nightmare!" Then, like a snake, I struck, hitting his neck with the precision of that snake. I began to drink, all the time he was trying to free himself. As I drank deeper he began to weaken and then fell limp. I continued to drink until his heart gave it's final beat. I removed my mouth from his neck and dropped his limp body back on the bed, saying, "Well, no one will have to fear you again!" I met Camaz outside the cell where he had just finished feeding. We kissed quickly and he said, "Well darling, did you get your fill?" "Yes, and he was so yummy!" Camaz laughed and saying, "Good, we need to get ready to try to save the king and queen! Astor has just gotten a lead on their location!" "Wonderful" I said and we headed back upstairs. An hour later we were back in the big SUV heading out of town. Everyone was armed and ready for battle. Astor had told us all of the details of where the king and queen were being held. Come to find out, they were abducted by a rouge band of vampires from the northern territories who were bent on taking over the southern states! Their plans were to use the ransom money to start a war! Camaz told me the king of New York had hired these rouges to kidnap the king and queen and was planning to kidnap us as well, to get money from Mexico! Boy were they going to be in for a surprise! As we traveled down the dark streets, I thought back to all of the training Camaz had given me on fighting. He had said I had become quite skilled at fighting, almost as good as he. I had been trained in all types of weaponry, including guns and swords. I couldn't wait to see how well my training is going to pay off. We arrived at the location where the reports had revealed the king and queen of Georgia were being held. The property was very run down and overgrown with vegetation. Camaz and Astor departed the SUV first and had a quick look around. The place appeared completely deserted, but our keen sense of smell told us otherwise. There were vampires, werewolves and many other creatures of the night there, along with humans! I got out of the SUV, went to Camaz's side and said, "Do you smell all of them? There are so many different creatures on this property!" "Yes my dear, I smell them. We must be prepared for anything!" Camaz grabbed my hand and we began our walk to the run down house. As we approached the doorway there was a very strong smell of werewolf. I looked at Camaz and said, "We are about to be attacked!" He pushed me behind him and shouted to the others, "Look out! Werewolves!!" As soon as the words left his mouth the door burst open and a pack of ten to twenty werewolves ran out toward us. I grabbed my sword from behind my back and prepared for the attack. My sword had been dipped in pure silver, a werewolf's worst nightmare! Camaz and Astor had already drawn their weapons and were shouting to the others, "See the large reddish colored one? He is the leader. Take him out and the others will run like the cowards they are!" The large reddish werewolf charged Camaz, snarling and brandishing his long white fangs. Camaz leapt straight up into the air just as the lead werewolf reached him, laughing as he went up. The werewolf leapt for him but Camaz was too fast. He hovered above the werewolf and then dove toward it with his sword drawn. With one swift slice he took the head of the werewolf and it tumbled to the ground. All of the other werewolves stopped in their tracks when they saw their leader destroyed. They turned and ran into the woods. Camaz walked up to me and said, "See, I told you they were all cowards without their leader!" I laughed and said, "And you were so right!" All of our friends rejoined us and we entered the house. The place was a pig sty! The furniture was broken and tattered but you could tell there were vampires and other creatures living in the house. Astor smelled the air and said, "My king and queen are here!" Camaz looked at Astor and asked, "Can you tell where they are being held?" Astor replied, "Yes, they are in the lower floors of the house's underground. This house used to be a plantation and the slave quarters are below. It is were they are being held." Slowly we began going through the house looking for the entrance to go below the house. We entered the kitchen and to the right of the big wood burning stove was the door we had been looking for. Astor pointed and said, "There. That is the way down to the slave quarters." We entered the doorway and started to descend the stairs into the lower quarters. I picked up a whiff of something strange. Something I had never encountered. I looked at Camaz and said, "What is that?" He looked at me and replied, "They have ghouls down there! Be very careful as they can do damage to a vampire just by biting them! It causes madness in a vampire! The only way to kill them is by cutting their head off!" So down into the darkness we went. I had always heard stories about supernatural creatures while growing up, but now I was getting up close and personal with these myths of my childhood. As we reached the bottom of the stairs, Camaz held his hand up for us to halt. He pointed to the left then the right of the stairwell letting us know the ghouls were lying in wait. I reached behind my back and retrieved my sword and readied myself for the attack. All at once they came rushing us from both sides! I had never seen anything so hideous in my life! Their skin was paper thin and greenish in color. Their eyes burned bright red. As Camaz and Astor rushed the ones coming at us I leapt into the air brandishing my sword and swinging as I came down, decapitating the ghoul in front of me. His head flew to one side and his limp body dropped to the ground. Camaz shouted "Look out!" I turned to see two ghouls running toward me. I thought to myself, "Oh shit!" I sprang straight up into the air. One of the ghouls managed to grab my right foot and yank me down to the ground. Before I could move, he was on top of me! Now I was fighting for my life! I had lost my sword and the only thing saving me from the ghoul biting me was my strength. I had been a vampire now for fifteen years, and as Camaz had told me when I was first made, I had become increasingly stronger over the years. The ghoul bared his teeth at me and hissed and said, "Hold still little vampire. I promise only a kiss for such a beautiful lady." He slowly began to lower his head toward my face. The entire time I was thinking, "Oh shit! I've got to get out of this mess. Madness is not my thing! While the ghoul was trying to bite me he wasn't paying attention to what was going on around him. Camaz was standing directly behind him and swung his sword taking the ghoul's head off. The body dropped down onto me and I pushed it to the side. Camaz reached down and picked me up saying , "Please baby, tell me you weren't bitten! I could not live with myself if I allowed that to happen." "No Camaz, he did not bite me. Sure as hell was trying though! You were right about me getting stronger with age!" As we looked around, our friends had finished off the rest of the ghouls. Camaz looked at me and said, "I told you they were the greatest warriors on the planet!" As we all grouped back together Astor announced, "There, through that door. I can smell the king and queen." I looked to Camaz saying, "I no longer smell any other vampires down here. Have they all left?" Camaz said, "I think once they saw us defeat the ghouls they ran off knowing we would destroy them as well. But I want you to stay here for now." Astor, Stantos and Camaz entered the room to the right of us. A few minutes later they emerged with two vampires, there clothing torn and muddy. They looked like they had not eaten in a month! The woman was very beautiful, with long flowing red hair and hazel eyes. The man was handsome, with very rugged features, but very subdued at the moment. Astor announced to us, "May I introduce King Jasper and Queen Victoria rulers of the southern nations." Everyone bowed except for Camaz and myself as we are above that being the king and queen of Mexico. Camaz spoke, "We are very pleased to meet you both. I am King Camaz and this is my Queen Anne. We are of the kingdom of Mexico." Camaz and Jasper shook hands. Jasper thanked us for saving them. Camaz said, "You're very welcome, but we must go now. I do not know if the others will be returning or not. Let's get you home." After returning the king and queen back to their home, we said our goodbyes and headed to our plane. It was time to go home for a much needed rest. But before we reached the plane we went on a hunt. Fighting werewolves and ghouls had made us extremely hungry.

Chapter 7

MY ABDUCTION

I muse, "It has been ten years since the kidnapping of the king and queen of Georgia. Camaz and I have been very happy just ruling our kingdom and loving each other. We have been together now going on 25 years and Camaz still makes love to me as if it was our first night together! Oh how I love this man!! I would lay down my life for him and he for me. Camaz has been call away for business in a near by town tonight, so I have decided to go hunting on my own. Camaz has always been with me during the hunt so this will be a first. I went to my closet and chose my most seductive outfit. I had the perfect body for attracting the must evil of men. My breast were ample and firm, my waist thin and my hips round and firm. My long legs went on forever. Camaz told me that, as a human, I had the most beautiful body he had seen in all of his 800 years, but my legs were what got him! The red dress I put on was very low cut,

showing off my ample breasts and short enough to reach just

below my crotch. The stilettos were six inch spikes with a pure

"come get me" look. I left the castle in my black BMW and

headed into town for my meal. I had heard there had been a

stalker/rapist the police had been trying to apprehend for the last

three months but they had not been able to locate him. Little did

I know that the man I would meet would turn out to be more

than a man! I left my car in a very seedy part of town as this

was where he had been reported doing his evil deeds. I began to

walk the street and smelled the air for my meal. I could smell

many evil men in the area, but after enjoying the one in Georgia

and remember how sweet his blood was, all I could do was

think about finding this man. Then I caught it, just a faint whiff,

but it was him! The smell was amazing and my throat began to

burn wildly. It took everything I had not to start running! So I

kept walking toward the wonderful scent, but as I walked the smell did not get any stronger. Strange, the smell should have been so strong that my killing instinct should have taken over. I continued to walk, scanning the air to see if the smell was leaving the area, but it was not! Suddenly a man jumped from the roof of a building I was in front of and landed in front of me. I stopped dead in my tracks and looked at the man. He was very handsome with roguish features and burning crimson eyes. A shiver went down my spine, for this was no man. This was a vampire! He grabbed my arm and said, "Good evening little vampire, are you looking for me?" I looked at him and said, "Why would I be looking for you? You are a vampire!" "The smell, little one, the one you are tracking, that is me!" "That is impossible! Vampires do not have that smell, only humans do!" "Oh, that is were you are wrong, little one. If a human that has done very evil things is bitten and changed a small amount of that smell stays with them!" I tried to pull away from the man, but he was to strong! "Do not resist me little one. I have lived for over 1000 years, you are no match for me." "Why are you doing this to me? I am not human, I am vampire!" "Yes you are and a very beautiful one at that. My name is Jack and I do believe your name is Anne, is it not?" I thought to myself, "Oh shit, he knows who I am." I screamed in my head as loud as I could, for you see, kings and queens have the ability to hear each other when they are in danger. So I screamed Camaz's name. Jack pulled me toward him and wrapped his arms around me. I yelled "Let go of me!" "Sorry little one, but I have so many plans for you!" He leapt up into the air and flew off with me. About thirty minutes later we landed in a field. There was a small cottage to the right of us. He looked at me and said, "Welcome to your new home, little one! I have dreamed of this day for the past ten years. Since I first saw you in Georgia!" I looked at him and said, "You were there?" "Yes, who do you think kidnapped the king and queen! My plan was going very well until your husband and his friends showed up. Now it is payback time." He started dragging me toward the cottage. I tried to resist but he was just to strong. We entered the house and he threw me on the couch. "Do not move from that spot little one. I do not want to kill you yet. I want to have some fun with you first. After I kill your husband. I know you have called for him, as I have said, I have been around for over 1000 years. I know that kings and queens can send out messages when they are in danger." He sat beside me, grinning and said, "Now we wait!" As time went by I thought to myself, "Alright Anne, how do we get out of this mess?" I knew my screams for help had reached Camaz and he was now tracking me. The vampire Jack, was more than 200 years older than Camaz. But I did not know how much stronger he could be. Camaz was very strong and well trained in the art of combat. I did not know if he would be bringing Dempie, his good friend and fierce fairy, with him. I could only hope he did. I didn't know if this Jack knew a vampire king and queen could feel when they were close to one another but I could feel Camaz getting closer. I could hear him screaming in my head, "I am coming my love, hold on I am almost there!" I scream back to him, "No Camaz, it is a trap! I am being held by the vampire who kidnapped the king and queen of Georgia. He is so evil! Please be careful!" The front door splintered and Camaz ran in. I shouted "Look out, Camaz. He is here and is going to try and kill you!" Jack stepped out of the shadows and said, "Hello Camaz, long time no see!" Camaz yelled at Jack, "If you have done anything to harm her, I will tear your head from your body!" "Oh, I have not done anything to her yet. First I will kill you and then the real fun will began!" Jack leapt toward Camaz, but Camaz is very quick and sidestepped him just in time, causing Jack to slam into the wall behind him. Jack leapt to his feet and ran at Camaz again. Camaz sidestepped him again. Camaz laughed loudly and said, "Oh, come on Jack, you can do better than that! You may be a few hundred years older than I am but you must remember, you were bitten, I was born to royals. I am much stronger and faster than you will ever be!" Suddenly the back door crashed open and in came Dempie and he was at my side in a protective stance. Camaz said, "Oh Jack, met my friend Dempie. Have you ever met a fairy before? Well, you will wish you hadn't when he is done with you if, you go anywhere near my wife! Now, shall we get this over with?" They began their dance of death. They circled each other then Jack leapt at Camaz and grabbed him around the neck. Camaz reached up, breaking Jack's hold and slinging him to the floor. Reaching behind, he retrieved his sword swung and in one quick stroke, took Jack's head from his shoulders. The body quivered then lay still. Camaz ran to me, pulling me into his arms kissing me madly and said, "I am so glad you are safe! I did not think we would make it here in time!" "Oh Camaz, I was so worried for you! I thought he would kill you being so much older! I would not be able to live without you!" "As I would not be able to live without you either. You are my life!" We hugged for a few more minutes and

left that terrible place. I was so ready to be back home!

Chapter 8

THE BIG SURPRISE

We arrived back at our palace the next evening around 10pm. Everyone was waiting for our return. Louisa came running to me, hugged me and stated, "Oh my queen, I am so glad you are okay and back with us!" I smiled at her and said, "Thank you Louisa, I am so happy to be back home!" She grabbed my hand and pulled me toward the staircase going to our upstairs quarters and said, "Come my queen, you are in need of a nice long, hot bath to relax you before you and the king go out for your dinner." We walked up the stairs and into Camaz's and my quarters. Louisa said, "Just have a seat and relax for a minute while I draw your bath." I went to my dressing table and sat down looking at myself in the mirror. There was blood and dirt all over my face from the fight with my abductor, Jack. I reached for my hair brush and began brushing the dirt and tangles from my hair, all the while remembering what I had

been through in the past forty-eight hours. I was so glad it was

over! Louisa came out of the bathroom to let me know my bath

was ready. I went into the bathroom, removed all dirty bloody

clothes and slipped into the wonderfully hot and perfumed

water. I had soaked for about forty-five minutes when I hear a

knock at the door, "Darling are you doing okay in there?" "Yes

Camaz, just relaxing for a little while." "Shall I come in and

wash your back for you?" "Yes my love, please do." By the time

he had finished a lot more had been done than a back wash.

After I had gotten dressed and bushed my hair out once more

Camaz asked, "Are you ready to go hunting my dear? I imagine

you are quite thirsty!" "Yes I am! The burn is beginning to

really bother me!" "Well then, we shall go and put out that fire!"

So off we went into the night looking for our next meal. We

went into the mountains because Camaz had gotten word a

madman was there killing men, women and children for no

reason other than the thrill of it. "Then we must go quickly and stop him before he can kill anymore innocents!" So we began searching the area for our killer. I smelled the air hoping to catch a whiff of the killer, but all I could smell was the sweet blood of innocents. Camaz looked at me and said, "There, that way, I think I have picked up something!" So we began running toward the woods. As we went deeper into the woods I began to smell the wonderful odor of pure evil. I dropped down into my hunting crouch and began letting my nose lead the way. As I tracked the wonderful smell Camaz was right beside of me. He whispered, "There, to the left, I can hear his strong heartbeat!" I stopped, listened, and said "Wait Camaz, there is another heartbeat as well!" So we crouched even lower and began creeping up to the area where the heartbeats were the strongest. There, in a clearing, we spotted the man. He had a small woman pinned to the ground and was raping her. I was appalled at what he was doing to the woman and all my muscles bunch ready for the attack. But Camaz stopped me and said "Wait, we must make sure no harm comes to the woman. We must get him off her before we can take him. Remember, we do not spill the blood of the innocent!" I looked at Camaz and said, "How will we stop him without hurting her?" Camaz pointed to an area on the other side of them and said, "When I have reached that spot I want you to wonder out into the opening and act like you are lost. Knowing he loves to rape and kill women he should come after you!" So I waited while Camaz positioned himself on the other side of the rapist. As soon as he reached the area, I stood up and began walking toward the two on the ground. The rapist heard me coming through the brush and jumped off of the woman. She was in really bad shape and unconscious. He walked toward me and said, "Hello there, are you lost?" I looked up at him and answered, "Yes sir, I was with some friends and we got separated. I am trying to find my way back into town." Then I looked toward the woman and said, "Hey, what is wrong with her? Is she alright?" "Yes, she is fine, just

sleeping" he lied. I watched as Camaz emerged from the woods

and ran to the woman, picked her up and ran back into the

woods. I thought to myself, "Good, now the games can began!"

The man reached for my arm. I looked at him and smiled,

bearing my glistening fangs. He stepped back and said, "What

the hell are you?" I laughed and said, "I am your worst

nightmare. We are going to play a little game of hide and seek

now. I will give you a five minute head start, then I am going to

find you. When I do, I am going to tear your arms and legs from

your body. Then I am going to take from you what you love

using the most! When I am done, while you lie ,bleeding to

death I am going to drink every last drop of blood left in your

body! Now run!!!" The man took off running into the woods as

fast as his legs could carry him. I went over to where Camaz

was with the woman. She was still out cold. Camaz said, "I am

going to take her down the mountainside to one of the homes

and leave her there. Someone will take care of her from there." I replied, "Okay, I will see you when you return. His five minutes are up and I am terribly hungry!" So, Camaz left carrying the woman and I headed off in the direction the man had run. He thought he could hide from me, but little does he know his blood was calling to me and I was able to track him down in a matter of seconds. He climbed high up a mighty oak tree and was hidden in the branches. I walked under the tree letting him think I did not see him. Then I turned and jumped straight up into the air and landed on the branch next to him. He screamed so loudly the sound echoed through the trees. When he stopped screaming, he pulled a knife from his belt and brandished it at me and said, "Stay away from me or I will kill you!" I laughed, "Sorry, but I don't think so, for you see, I am already dead! I am a vampire and I am going to make you pay for all of the horrible things you have done in your lifetime!" I leapt at him and grabbed him. He tried to stab me but the knife couldn't penetrate my stone hard skin. I yanked him from the tree branch and jumped down to the ground on top of him. I had broken his back in the fall and he couldn't move. I looked down at him and said, "I told you I was going to rip your limbs from your body first and take that dick you are so proud of and so I shall." I grabbed both of his arms and yanked, ripping them from his body. He began screaming and shrieking. I took his legs next, laughing as the flesh tore from the bones. Then I reached for the prize and ripped his dick from his body. As he lay bleeding I looked into his dying eyes and said "Now, as I promised, I am going to drain you dry!" I pushed his head to one side and struck. His sweet blood began flowing over my lips, down my throat and I drank until he was dry. I rolled off him and lay there for a moment, savoring the sweetness of his blood. Camaz returned a few minutes later and we headed for home.

Chapter 9

DREAMS OF HOME

For almost twenty years I had lived with my beloved Camaz as his wife and queen. But the last few of those years I had been dreaming of going back home. I missed my beloved country and was very home sick! One night while we were hunting, Camaz looked at me and asked, "What is bothering you my dear?" I looked up into those deep green eyes and said, "I have become very home sick these last few years and would like to go back to America for a visit. I know I cannot see any of my family but I would like to just go home and be close to them if at all possible!" Camaz smiled gently at me and said, "If you need to go home for a visit then I shall take you home!" The next day we started making plans for the trip to America. I was very excited about going home! I missed my family so much. My mother and father had grown old over the years and did not have much time left. I knew I would not be able to see them in person, but at least I could see them from afar! The same of my brothers and sister. William and Robert were 59 and 62, Elise had just turned 54. I had not seen any of my family in twenty years, so I had no idea what they looked like. I couldn't show myself to them for I was dead to them. They were told I had been killed in a car crash. When they had my funeral I had to lie very still in the coffin and pretend I was dead. After the funeral and burial Camaz had come to the cemetery, dug me up and we went back to Mexico. Two days later we were on our private plan heading to the states. My hometown was in New Jersey, so was going to take a few hours to get there. I had picked up a new book about vampires and I was reading it as we flew. It was a really good book. It was about a young girl who meets a boy in high school and they fall in love. She finds out he is a vampire but does not care because she is in love with him. But those vampires were not like us, they could go out in the daylight and they only hunted animals. Animal blood has no

appeal to us because they are innocents. They only kill to live. A

few hours later we arrived at the Philadelphia Airport and went

to the rental desk to pick up our car. Camaz was not familiar

with the area so I drove. As I was driving everything was so

beautiful, even though it was dark I could see perfectly, as if it

was daytime. We arrived in my hometown of Bridgeton about

an hour later. I drove down Broad Street looking at all of the

buildings remembering everything of my youth. Going to Broad

Street school as a child, then Bridgeton Middle School and High

school. I had just graduated from high school and was in

Mexico as my graduation gift when I met Camaz. My parents

lived on Albertson Avenue, right across the street from my

old high school. I remembered rushing home from school every

day just so I could watch the vampire soap opera Dark Shadows

with Barnabas Collins. Boy do I miss that show! As we

approached my old school I said to Camaz, "That is the high

school I went to right before I met you back in 1974. Hard to believe it has been 25 years already! Seems like we just met yesterday!" Camaz replied, "I know my dear, every day with you is like the first!" We turned onto Albertson Avenue and parked at the bottom of the hill and walked to the top. I could see my house and, if I had still able to cry, I would. All of the happy memories came flooding back. At a little after 3am, all of the homes were dark. We reached my house and I leapt to the second floor balcony where my old room was located. I listened to see if anyone was occupying my old room but I heard nothing. I used to sneak out when I was a teenager, so I knew how to get into my room. I removed the screen from the window and pushed gently. The window slid up easily. I stepped inside the room and looked around. Everything was as I had left it! Mom and Dad had not changed anything! It was as if they still expected my return. I quietly opened the bedroom door and stepped out into the hallway. I could hear their breathing coming from their bedroom. Camaz had stayed back in my

room and was looking at my things. I knew I should not be

doing it, if they awoke and found me there I might have scared

them to death. But all I wanted to do was look upon the faces of

my parents. No one else was living in the house, so their

bedroom door was open. I quietly entered the room and went to

the bedside to look down at my sleeping parents. The years

showed in their faces, my parents were then in their late 80s, but

they still were a beautiful sight! I stood there watching them

sleep for a few more minutes and then quietly left the room. If

my heart were still beating it would skip a beat. I am was so

happy. I returned to my old room and Camaz was sitting at my

desk looking at my yearbook. He looked up at me and smiled

saying, "My dear, you are as beautiful now as you were back

then!" I answered softly, "Why thank you kind sir!" Camaz

reminded me that it was getting late and he was quite thirsty. So

we left my parent's home and headed out into the night in

search of our next meal. After our meal we found a near by cemetery and entered one of the mausoleums to sleep. You could tell no one had been in the place for many years, so we knew we were safe. We laid down and fell into the sleep of death. When we awoke the following evening, we returned to the airport and headed back home.

Chapter 10

VAMPIRES HAVE BABIES!

One night after our hunt we were lying in bed and I rolled over and asked, "When I was kidnapped and you were fighting with Jack, the rapist vampire, you said something to him I do not understand," Camaz looked at me and asked, "What is that my dear?" "You said he was a made vampire and you were born. I did not know vampires could have offspring?" Camaz smiled at me and said, "Only royals can produce children. My father was a royal so he and my mother produced me." I cocked my head to one side and asked, "So you are capable of having children as long as you mate with another royal?" "That is correct, my dear, my mother and father were both royals, but their marriage was arranged. I chose to turn and marry a human. That is my right." "So your line ends with you?" "Yes my dear, why are you so concerned?" "But what if something

happens to you? There would be no one to carry on your line!"
"Do not worry love, nothing is going to happen to me." "You
don't know that Camaz! You should have chosen a royal for your
bride!" "I chose you and that is all that matters to me! Now, we
will not speak of this anymore. Come here, I have something for
you." Camaz pulled me toward him and took me into his arms.
His hands began to caress my body sending shivers of delight
down my spine. We made love for several hours, for vampires do
not get tired. As dawn approached I drifted off to sleep in my
loving husband's arms. The next evening when we woke we
were told our friend, Astor, had come for a visit and wished to
speak to Camaz. He kissed me on my forehead and told me he
would be back soon and we would go hunting. As I laid in the
bed I thought about what we had discussed the previous evening.
Camaz was the last of his line and without an heir, there would
be no more of his bloodline to rule this country. I knew I was
not capable of producing his heir, that only a royal could do that,

but there must have been some way to keep his bloodline going. While we were hunting I would ask him more about siring an heir, even if it means going to another woman! Camaz returned about an hour later and let me know Astor would be staying with us for a few weeks. He had business here to take care of. He asked me if I minded if Astor went hunting with us. I said, "I don't mind, but I do need to talk to you about something. But it can wait until we return from the hunt." So we all went into the beautiful summer night in search of our meal. After the hunt we returned to the castle, said out good nights to our friend, Astor, and went upstairs to our room. Once in our room I told Camaz I needed to discuss something with him and we sat down to talk. I began, "Camaz I know you said having an heir does not matter to you, but it matters to me. I have been doing a lot of thinking and I think you should find a royal female to mate with." Camaz looked at me strangely and said, "My dear, do you understand what you are asking of me? In order for me to produce a heir, I must have sex with another woman. Will you be able to handle it?" "If it will allow your bloodline to continue, yes I would. I need to know she will be a surrogate mother and not involved in our lives after the child is born. The child would be ours." Camaz thought for a minute and replied, "I am not sure if such a thing is possible. I will have to talk with the council. Most royals are wed before a child is even considered. I will talk with them when we rise tomorrow evening." As I drifted off to sleep I thought It would be nice to have a child to raise with Camaz. But would I be able to love the child knowing it came from a union between him and another woman? But then I thought, "Well it would be the same as if we were a human couple that could not have children and had to use a surrogate." But nothing could be for sure until Camaz talked with the council, so I left it at that. The next evening when we woke we got dressed and headed to the council's chambers. They were all present when we arrived. We stood before them and Camaz said, "Good evening council.

We have come to you to find out if something is possible."

"What is it you wish of us, sire?" asked Gabriel head council member. "My wife has learned that in order for my bloodline to continue I must mate with a royal. She has agreed to allow this but we do not know if it is possible. The royal must be a surrogate and have nothing to do with the child after it is born. We will be the ones to raise the child. Is this at all possible?" Gabriel and the other council members got together and discussed the issue. After about 20 minutes Gabriel returned and said, "It is possible sire, but we must find a royal female who is willing to leave her child. This is a very rare thing and has only happened once in over 1000 years. We will send messengers to all of the countries with the invitation to all of the royal females. We will have to wait for a reply." We thanked the council for their time and consideration on the issue and left. Camaz said to me, "So, now, my dear, all we can do is wait. Are you sure this is what you want to do?" "Yes, love, I am positive."

Chapter 11

PRINCESS SURROGATE

After waiting almost a month we finally got word back from the council. They had located a royal female willing to conceive and carry Camaz's heir. Her name was Princess Katrina of Brazil. She was to arrive in two weeks, so much planning needed to be done. She had signed a contract with our council agreeing to relinquish the child when it was born. She was to be paid a diary of one million US dollars. The council explained she had no plans of wedding a royal as she had fallen in love with a mortal and planned to change him, as Camaz had changed me. Camaz explained to me a vampire only carries the child for a little over a month and then gives birth. Vampire children grow very fast and reach adulthood in three human years. While he was explaining this to me, I just sat there staring in disbelief! Our child would become an adult in three years! He also explained once the child is born a special ceremony will be preformed by the council making me the child's mother. So, all we could do at that point was await for the princess' arrival. I just hoped she was nice. After about two weeks Princess Katrina arrived at our place. She was stunning! She had long flowing black hair and eyes the color of honey. Her skin tone was a light olive color just like Camaz's. She spoke in a very refined tone. We all met at the council's chambers and began planning the date of conception. Then something very strange happened to me, I began to feel very jealous of her! She would be sleeping with my man! Camaz tried to set my mind at ease, reminding me this was my idea and if I could not bare the idea of him being with her we would call the whole thing off. I told Camaz it just killed me that I could not give him the heir he needed and the jealousy was just because of that. But deep down I could not bear the thought of him being inside of another woman! But I knew we needed to have this happen. So I sucked it up and the conception went on as planned. Camaz explained to me female royals are very fertile and it would only take one mating for her to become pregnant. The date was in five days and he would take her somewhere I would not be. He would only be gone for one night, so I agreed. Camaz made me promise not to go hunting alone as he did not want anything to happen to me like the last time. So I agreed to take Dempie the fairy with me. I knew he would not let any harm come to me. Camaz and Katrina returned to the palace after the planned date and announced all had gone well. Katrina was pregnant and the baby was due in a month. She was given a suite on the third floor of the palace and several ladies-in-waiting to care for her. I was told when the time came for the birth that she will ask to be left alone. Vampires give birth on their own, without any help. From what I had been told, it is a very private and special time for the mother-to-be. Once she had given birth she would announce the arrival of the child and turn him or her over to us and leave.

Following weeks I had gotten to know Katrina very well. We had become very good friends. I spent a lot of time talking with her. Then one day I went to her room to speak to her and was told she was not seeing anyone. Her time had come. So we waited for the birth of our heir. The night of the birth, Camaz and I had gone out hunting and had just returned to the palace when my lady-in-waiting approached us very excited. She proclaimed, "Sires great news! The child has arrived and it is a boy! Katrina has asked to see the queen first." I raced up to the third floor where Katrina's suite was located and knocked on her door. She asked who it was and I answered, "It is Anne. Louisa said you wanted to see me." "Yes, please come in Anne." I entered the room and she was on the big bed in the center of the room. She said, "Come, my good friend, and see your new son." I walked over to the bedside and looked down into the face of an angel. He had his father's beautiful emerald eyes and Katrina's jet black hair. His small body was perfect. I asked,

"May I hold him?" She replied, "Of course you can, he is your son now!" I reached down, picked him up and cradled him in my arms. He looked up at me and smiled! He already had a full set of milky white teeth and little fangs. I looked at Katrina and said, "Oh my, he is absolutely perfect!" She smiled at me and said, "Yes he is, and he looks just like his father! May I ask what you will name him?" "Camaz and I have discussed what we will name the child if it was a boy and have decided on Mikal." "Oh what a wonderful name." she replied. There came a knock at the door and Camaz asked, "May I come in?" Katrina replied, "Yes, Sire, please do." Camaz walked into the room and came over to where we were sitting. I was still holding Mikal and I said, "Look, my love, he is perfect! He has your beautiful green eyes!" Camaz looked down on the child and smiled the most beautiful smile I had ever seen. I could tell he had already fallen in love with his son! Katrina stayed for a few more days then returned to Brazil. We had made a nursery out of the room adjoining ours and Mikal had settled in nicely. I knew I

was going to love motherhood!

Chapter 12

MIKAL'S COMING OF AGE

It had been 2 ½ years since Mikal's birth and he had grown into a fine young teenager! He was tall and muscular just like his father. We had done everything together as a family including the hunt. Mikal had learned very well in both the hunt and fighting skills. He had very good teachers with all of Camaz's royal guard helping in the training. In 6 months he would reach full adulthood and the council would proclaim him prince and heir to the kingdom. The year was 2001 and it turnede out to be a very bad year for the whole world. A very evil man had attacked the United States and killed thousands of people. Everyone was trying to find him and destroy him including the vampire kingdoms! He would be a great prize for any vampire who captured him because his blood would be priceless! So that was when our son deceived once the council proclaimed him an adult he would go in search of this evil man. On our son's

third birthday he left home. I was very upset at him for many

days for leaving us, but I had to let him go, he was an adult now.

We heard from Mikal every few days with a progress report

on his hunt for this man. He had taken a few of his closest

friends and warriors with him. They were somewhere in

Afghanistan. One night he called and as we were talking he

told me he was very close to finding the man and when he

did he planned on capturing him and bringing him back here. I

asked him why and he said, "My dearest mother, he shall be a

gift for you and father!" I was so proud of our son! After

speaking to him a few more minutes he told me he had to go.

They had just gotten a lead on his prey's whereabouts. He told

me he would call again as soon as he had news of the capture.

We said our goodbyes and hung up. This made me very sad. I

missed him so much and worried about his safety all of the time.

Camaz had reassured me, saying Mikal would be fine but I

could not help worrying! A few days later Mikal called to let us know he had captured the man and was returning to the palace. I got with Louisa and my other ladies-in-waiting and planned a big surprise party for Mikal. We had the finest killers imported from all over the world for his pleasure. We also invited the most available royal females in the world. Mikal had come to the age to choose his bride and future queen. But just like his father he had the choice of a vampire or human bride. One night after our hunt I asked Camaz, "Do you think he will choose a vampire royal? He knows the story of his birth and that I was bitten not born." Camaz looked at me lovingly and replied, "I do not know what choice our son will make, but I do know I made the right choice!" He took me into his arms and kissed me and made passionate love to me for the next several hours. The following evening, when we arose, I told Camaz I had some errands to run and would be back. I left and went into town. I wanted to find Mikal the perfect homecoming present. I knew he was into all types of weaponry and there was a small

weapon shop in town. I walked into the shop and began to look

around when a elderly man came up to me and asked if he could

help. I explained I was looking for a homecoming gift for my

son and he loved old swords. The man told me he had some

very old and beautiful swords and offered to show them to me.

He stated they were very valuable and were kept in the back of

the store. I said, "Sure,I would love to look at them." He was a

very nice man and I could not smell any evil in him so, without

thinking, I followed him into the back room where he kept the

swords. When we were in the back of the building we entered a

small room where there were many old weapons. He led me

over to a showcase displaying the sword he had told me about. I

looked down, It was silver with very intricate etchings on the

handle and blade. It looked like it was from the 14th century. I

asked him the cost of the blade and he said the price was

$5800.00. I found a beautiful leather sheath for the blade as well. I had him box up the sword, paid him and headed back home. While I was driving back I noticed a woman on the side of the road. She had been beaten, raped and was barely alive. I leapt from the car, running up to her and gently lifted her into my arms. I carried her back to the car and headed for the local hospital. She was bleeding very badly and I could smell her sweet, salty blood. It caused my throat to burn but not in the usual way. It called to me. I tried to resist but the pull was getting stronger! Thank God we were at the hospital or I don't know what I would have done to that poor woman. Camaz had said we only drink the blood of the very evil but there was just something about her blood that called to me. I took her into the hospital, nurses came and took her away. The woman at the desk asked me if I knew the woman and I told her no, that I had found her on the side of the road. She asked me a few more questions and then I left. The urge to stay was so strong! I wanted this woman's blood more than I had every wanted a human's blood before! I was so confused! When I reached the

palace I went straight to our room looking for Camaz. He had to

explain to me what had happened to me! But he was not there. I

went downstairs and into the library where I found him with

Astor. I approached them and told what had happened, how I

had wanted the woman. They explained to me we crave all

human blood but choose to only kill the evil ones and that once

in a while a vampire will run into a human whose blood is so

powerful it will call to them. Camaz told me he was so proud of

me for resisting killing the woman. He said it is a very hard

thing to do when the blood calls to you. I told Camaz we needed

to go back to where I found the woman and try to track her

attacker. Astor asked if we minded if he came with us. We told

him he was welcome to hunt with us. About thirty minutes later

we arrived at the spot where I had found the woman. It had

rained earlier so most of her blood had been washed away, but I

could still pick up on it! We began walking the area where I found the woman, smelling the air for her attacker. We were not having any luck and then I caught a whiff of something. I closed my eyes and let my senses take over. I hissed in a low voice, "Over there!" I dropped down into my hunting crouch and began to follow the smell. So the hunt began. I arrived in a small clearing with Camaz and Astor right behind me. The smell was getting much stronger! My throat began to burn wildly and I was so thirsty! I spotted a small building to the right of the clearing and there was smoke coming from the chimney. I pointed to the building and said, "There! In there. I can smell him! He is so evil, the woman was not the first he had attacked but she is the first to live." I explained I want to go into the building first and they needed to wait outside for me. This man was going to pay with his life! I was not dressed in my must provocative hunting outfit but I still looked good. I walked up to the door and knocked. The man came to the door and asked, "How can I help you?" "I ran out of gas about a mile back and was looking or a phone. Do you have one I can use?" As I looked up at him and smiled, not enough to show my fangs. He looked me up and down. I could almost hear the wheels turning in his evil mind. He answered, "Sure, come on in. I have a phone you can use." I walked into the building and closed the door behind me. The man said, "Come on. It is just in the other room." We walked into the next room and he pointed and said, "It is over there." I turned and walked toward the phone, putting a little extra sway in my hips. The next thing I knew the man had grabbed me and was trying to drag me to the ground. I played his game and screamed. He slapped me in the face so hard that if I had still been human he would have broken my jaw! I fell down, on purpose, and allowed him to get on top of me. He said, "Do not struggle or I will kill you." He started to undress me and began fondling my firm breast. I could see the lust building in his eyes. I looked up at him and grinned widely, baring my fangs for him to see. He froze and said,

"What the hell are those?" I laughed and said, "Why, my dear, they are my fangs. How else could I feed!" I yanked him down to me and struck, drained him dry.

Chapter 13

MIKAL'S HOMECOMING

A few days later Mikal returned home with his prize. The man looked to be middle eastern and very rugged. Mikal took the man down to our special rooms where we kept all of the vintage drinks. He locked the man in a cell and came back up to see us. He hugged me and said, "Good evening Mother, I have missed you!" "As I have missed you, my son!" He asked, "How have things been while I was gone? Everything is okay, I hope." Camaz replied, "Yes, son, things have been very quit here." I lead Mikal to the couch and we sat down. "We have arranged a homecoming ball in your honor and have invited all of your friends. We have also sent out invitations to all of the available royal females in the world. Some have already arrived. We will not ask you to choose if you are not ready, just meet them and see if any of them interest you." Mikal replied, "I will meet these women, but I am not ready to settle down yet." "That is your choice my son." "Now, I have a very special gift for you!" I reached beside the couch and retrieved the box containing the sword. I handed it to him and smiled"Welcome home Son!" Mikal opened the box and saw the leather sword sheath and smiled. He removed the sword from it's sheath and said, "Oh Mother, it is so beautiful! Thank you very much." I smiled and said, "When I saw it in the shop I just knew you would love it!" We shared a glorious hug. Two days later everything was in readiness for Mikal's homecoming ball. All of the guests had arrived and were seated in the Great Hall. There was a total of eight royal females lined up on one side of the hall. They were all very beautiful and dressed in their finest apparel. Camaz and I took our seats at the royal table, along with Astor and Dempie. We announced to the crowd that we welcomed them all and to enjoy the festivities. The music began to play and Camaz reached for my hand and asked, "Will you do me the honor of the first dance, My Love?" I giggled and said "Of course, your Majesty. I would follow you anywhere and do anything for you!" He kissed me and led me onto the dance floor. As he held me close, I thought, "God, I still love this man with my entire heart and soul, even after all these years!" While we were dancing I looked over to where the girls were and noticed Mikal speaking to one of them. She was very petite and delicate. He seemed very interested in her. He took her hand and led her onto the dance floor. I smiled up at Camaz and said, "Looks like our little prince has found his princess!" Camaz smiled and said, "Yes it does, my dear." After the dance I said, "Dear, I am very thirsty shall we go sample the rare vintages downstairs?" After you, my dear," he replied. After dinner we said our good nights and got ready to take the sleep of death. Before we left the room we noticed Mikal was still with the young woman he had danced with earlier. Her name was Iris and she was from America. She was the same age as Mikal and they seemed to be getting along very well. We walked over to them to say our good nights and Mikal said he was going to stay up a little longer with Iris and he kissed me on my forehead. I said, "Goodnight my son, we will see you tomorrow evening." We woke the next evening and went to the living room. We were greeted by Mikal and Iris. They were waiting to speak with us. Mikal began, "Mother, Father, we would like to ask your permission to begin the courting ritual." We smiled at them and said in unison, "You have our permission to begin courting." They smiled and said thank you. Then they left the room. I smiled at Camaz and said, "Oh darling, looks like we may be planning a wedding soon!" He replied, "That it does my dear, that it does!" Later that night was when I found out once our son weds they would become the new king and queen and we would have to leave. I said to Camaz, "Really? But where

will we go?" He smiled at me and said, "That is entirely

up to you, my dear!" Mikal and Iris's courtship lasted only six

months. They asked for our blessing, for them to wed. So

the wedding plans began and our departure was planned. We

would be going back to America!

Chapter 14

LIVING IN AMERICA

It was the beginning of June, 2013, Camaz and I were living in the mountains of North Carolina. He said they reminded him of home. We had been there for almost ten years. I had been a vampire for forty-nine years. I was still considered very young in vampire years, considering Camaz is 858. Mikal and Iris were ruling Mexico and were madly in love. They had two children so far, Kristen was born first, then Samuel. They were all here for a visit. It was so wonderful seeing them. The children were almost fully grown and would be going off on their own soon. Kristen wanted to be a painter, so she was going to college that fall. Samuel was in his final year of high school and had not yet deceived what he wanted to do. He had met a very nice girl in school and they had been dating for three months. Her name was Kimberly, but she preferred Kim. She had come along with them for the visit. She was not aware of what Samuel was, but I felt she suspected. She was a very smart girl, she reminded me of myself when I was her age. They were down at the lake swimming, at around 9pm when I suggested to Camaz we go out and hunt. I was very thirsty and I had picked up a scent that I just had have! We said our good byes to everyone and let them know we were going into town for a date night. We couldn't tell them where we were going actually because of Kim. So we went in search of our next meal. As I stalked through the woods with Camaz at my side I stopped and tested the air. I could smell the wonderfully sweet and pungent odor of my dinner. I dropped into my hunting crouch and began to follow the smell. We came upon a clearing and noticed a tent in the southern corner. I looked up at Camaz, smiled saying, "Oh my, doesn't he smell sweet?" Camaz smiled at me and said,

" Yes, indeed he does! I smell another one in the woods. I am

going after him. Enjoy your dinner, love!" Then he was gone. I

began walking slowly up to the tent and called out, "Is anyone

here that can help me? I am lost!" The man came out of the tent

and looked me up and down with a look that said I could eat

you right now. I laughed to myself as I thought that it would be

me eating him. I was completely full and waiting for Camaz to

return. He came through the clearing smiling and saying, "My

dear, you are positively glowing. He must have been delicious!"

I replied, " Oh yes! That was one of the best meals I have had in

ages!" Camaz came and sat beside of me and began rubbing my

back. I stared into his eyes and said, "The wonderful meal has

made me hungry for you, my king!" He laid me down in the

grass and began removing my dress. When we were both

undressed, he looked at me lovingly and said, " You are so

beautiful! You are my life, my love, my queen!" He began

kissing me, our bodies intertwining in the moonlight. As I

reached my orgasm, I screamed out his name over and over.

"God I love this man!" We arrived back at the cabin around 4am

and went inside to get ready for our sleep of death. Everyone

was up except for Kim, who I could hear deep in sleep in the

next room. We said our good nights and headed to our room.

The next evening we woke to a knock at our door. It was

Samuel. He was very upset and needed to talk to us. We told

him to give us a few minutes, to get dressed and we would be

right out. When we got to the living-room we asked, " What's

wrong?" Samuel answered, "Kim is missing. I have looked

everywhere but cannot find her!" I asked, " Did you guys have

a fight?" Samuel looked down at his feet and answered, " No. I

told her last night I want to marry her. And then, I told her what

we are. When I got up she was gone. I thought she had taken

what I had told her pretty well. But I guess not." Samuel looked so sad I just had to go over and hug him. I said, " Dear, if she really loves you she will come back. She needs some time to let everything sink in." "I hope so, grandmother. I do not know what I will do if I lose her!" "Don't worry Samuel, give her some time. She will come back I promise!" A few hours later there was a knock at the door. I opened it and saw Kim. I asked her in and offered her a seat. We all sat down at the table and she began to speak. " Is it true what Samuel has told me? Are you really vampires?" She looked down at her hands when she asked her question. I reached for her hands and said, " Yes my dear, it is true. But like you, I was once human. I met Camaz forty-nine years ago and fell in love with him. I knew we were meant to be together and the very next night I allowed him to make me immortal. But, as with me, it is your decision to make. If you love Samuel and do not want to be with anyone else then that is the way it should be." Kim looked at me with tears in her eyes and said, "I do love him, with all of my heart and there can be no other, but I am afraid! I do not want to kill people like you do!" I smiled at her and said, "My dear, there is no need to be afraid of that! We only kill the most evil of all the humans and only take the ones we need to survive! If you choose our way of life we will teach you how to do this as Camaz taught me so many years ago. I have never taken the blood of an innocent and neither have any of our coven." Kim wiped her eyes and smiled at me." I want to spend the rest of my life with Samuel and as long as I do not have to kill innocent people then I want to become like you!" "There is one thing I must tell you before you make your decision. When you become a vampire, you will not be able to have children. This is something you need to consider long and hard!" "But Anne, you have children!" "Yes my dear, but my children are not from my womb. They are from another born royal female vampire. At first I did not like the idea of Camaz being with another woman, but I so wanted to have children and Camaz needed an heir. It was my idea, not his." She looked at me quizzically and said, " I have never thought about having children, so it doesn't matter to me." "Then I suggest you sleep on it tonight and make sure this is what you want. If you do decide to accept our gift we will not change you until you have finished high school." Kim smiled at me and said she would and went to her room. Samuel allowed Kim her privacy knowing she had a big decision to make.

Chapter 15

KIM'S GRADUATION

Well, the time had finally came. Kim's graduation day! I was so excited to see her graduate! We had arrived in Mexico the night before and had just gotten up. Because we could not go out during the day to watch the commencement, they had been recorded for us to watch. Samuel and Kim were waiting for us in the viewing room and were very excited. Samuel smiled at us and said, " Kim has made her decision and has agreed to become my wife!" I went up and hugged them,saying, " Oh, I am so happy for both of you! When is the happy day?" "We have deceived on an August wedding, after the honeymoon Kim will be changed." I looked at them and said, "After the honeymoon? You do understand you cannot have a real honeymoon like humans? That sex is not possible until Kim has been changed. Please tell me you understand this!""Yes

grandmother, we understand. I want Kim to have the best of

both worlds before I change her."Camaz spoke, " You two must

understand. Being physical is a very powerful thing for a

vampire. You can lose your self-control during sex and kill her.

Please tell me you do understand this Samuel. Once you are

married and alone you will want her more than you have ever

wanted her. If you become intimate it will cause your blood to

boil and you will have no control. It might be better to change

her on your wedding night. The transformation takes a little

over two days and then you can be together in all ways."

"Grandfather, I understand your concern, but it will be okay. We

have agreed to wait until after she has been changed." "I just

hope you know what you are doing. I would hate for you to hurt

or kill her. You would never forgive yourself. I had wanted your

grandmother from the first day I laid eyes on her but I knew the danger if I had not waited for the change." "I understand your

concerns grandfather, but I promise it will be okay." Later that

evening, while we were out hunting, I asked Camaz if he

thought the kids would wait. He told me how hard it had been

for him to wait but it had been well worth the wait. But he did

not know if they could abstain for a week after they were

married. He then told me the story of Maria, a young woman he

had met back in 1872. He had lusted after this woman and she

had wanted him as well. He had not told her what he was and

they had began having sex when he lost control. He said he had

never had sex before so he did not know what would happen.

Before he could stop himself the fire in his blood had taken

over and he killed her. From that night on he swore he would

never have sex with a mortal again. He told me the night we had

went to dinner, so many years ago, he had wanted me so badly

the fire had almost taken him over again. But something inside him was stronger than the fire and had taken hold of him. He told me if his heart could still beat it would have skipped a beat and that was when he knew he truly loved me. After we arrived at the house, I went to our room to ready myself for the sleep of death. While I was preparing, I began thinking to myself, "Could we trust the kids not to have sex while they where on their honeymoon?" After the story Camaz told me about Maria, I did not think so. I knew how much they loved each other and I knew how strong the urge could be when you want someone that much. I had wanted Camaz to make love to me so badly the night before he changed me, my body ached for him. I knew Kim had to have been feeling the same way about Samuel. So I decided to speak with her alone before the wedding. If anything were to happen to her I would never forgive myself as I really loved this girl! Camaz entered the room and came up to me, rubbed my shoulders and said, "What is worrying you, dear one?" I looked up at him and replied, " I am just worried about the children. I am so afraid for them! What if he lets the blood lust take over and kills her! Isn't there something we can do?" "I understand your concern, my love, but we cannot interfere in this. This is something they must do on their own." "But what if he kills her? He will never forgive himself!" Camaz placed his hand on my face and said, "I know my dear, I have the same concern myself. You have such a good and gentle heart, but we cannot interfere." As we laid down for our deep sleep, Camaz took me into his arms and held me to his chest. He whispered in my ear, "Sleep now, my love, for we have a busy evening tomorrow. We have a wedding to plan." I rolled onto my side and said, "My love, I am not ready for sleep! I need you!!" He chuckled under his breath and said, " You never cease to amaze me! Is that all I am to you? A sex toy!" I pulled him closer to me and showed him just what a great sex toy he was! A few hours later we fell into our deep sleep, both of us with smiles on our

faces! God how I loved that man!!

Chapter 16

WEDDING PREPARATIONS

It was the first of August and I was busy with the wedding

plans along with Samuel's mother. The wedding and reception

were to be held here, at our house, and was only three weeks

away. I had been busy arraigning the flower delivery and

working on all the seating for the reception. Our werewolf

friends took care of everything that needed to be done during the

day and we were almost done. Kim, Iris and I had an

appointment one evening for the final fittings of our dresses.

Kim's gown is was beautiful! It reminds me a little of mine.

She was so stunning that when Samuel saw her he wasn't able to

take his eyes off of her! I just wished Kim's parents could have

been there to see their little girl get married, but unfortunately

they were killed in an accident several years before. Her uncle,

Charles, her father's brother, would be giving her away. She had

asked her best friend, Lisa, to be her maid of honor and Samuel

had ask his best friend and werewolf buddy, Raul, to be his best

man. They grew up together and Raul was a fierce and loyal

friend. The evening before the wedding everything was going

smoothly. Camaz, Samuel, Iris, Mikel and I were all out hunting

so we would not need to hunt the night of the wedding. We

heard on the local news the day before there had been a killing

spree a few counties away. So we had deceived to go and take

care of the problem. A good thing too, because I was starving!

We had taken to the air to get there quicker. In about an hour we

arrived in the small town of Sunburst. But where to start

looking? The reports had stated thirty women and children had

disappeared in the woods outside of Saddle Creek within the last

three months. Sunburst Woods was a popular camping site in the

North Carolina mountains. The reports said the men of the

families had came back from either fishing or hunting to find

their campsites empty and their families where no were to be

found. I was very familiar with the area as I grew up there when

I was a child. I told everyone to follow me as I had an idea

where to look for whoever had taken the humans. There was an

area high up in the mountainside where there were caves. It only

took us a few minutes to reach the site. There was a strong smell

of dead blood in the area. I stopped and smelled the air for the

distinctive aroma of our prey. I caught it and pointed to a small

cave opening. When we reached the opening I stopped short,

there was something else there besides our prey. There was also

the smell of the blood of a living human innocent. I whispered

to Camaz, "Do you smell that? Someone is still alive! We must

hurry, they may be running out of time!" So we ran, like the

wind, into the cave and emerged in in a large opening. There we

saw two small children and a woman huddled together. To the

right of them were many bodies, mangled and mutilated. From a dark corner of the cavern, four men appeared and yelled, "Who the hell are you!" I looked my target in the eyes and said, " I am the thing of your nightmares. The thing you fear the most. DEATH!" I ran toward the man and pounced on him, knocking him to the ground. I was aware of the others taking care of the other three men, but I did not care, my thrust had taken control of my body. I stuck at the man's throat. He screamed in terror. I felt his sweet blood begin to flow over my lips and tongue before I really lost it. I started to rip the him apart while I was still attached to his neck. When I came back to my senses, I looked at what was left of the man and backed away horrified! Camaz was quickly by my side and asked, " My dear, are you okay? You look so frightened!" I answered, my voice shaking "What happened to me? I started to drink and I lost it! I tore him apart and didn't even know I was doing it! Camaz, what is wrong with me?!" Camaz was silent for a moment then

answered, "Do you remember when I told you the story of

Maria and how she had died?" I shook my head. He continued,

" I think the blood lust took you over in the same way!" "But

Camaz I did not lust after this man! You are the only man I have

ever lusted for! Why would I do this?!" He pulled me into his

chest hugged me tightly and said, " I know, my love. I think

your lust was for his blood not his body. Remember when you

told me about the woman you found on the side of the road and

how much you had wanted her? I think that is what happened

with this man and you did to him what you couldn't do to her." I

thought for a moment and he was right! I had wanted the

woman so badly but I did not want to kill an innocent. This man

was no innocent I looked at Camaz and smiled. " Darling you

are so right. That is how I felt about the woman but she was

a innocent and I couldn't take her life but I could take his!" We went to the woman and children and asked if they were okay.

The woman looked at us and said, "I don't know what you

are and I do not care, you have saved our lives! Thank you!!" I

smiled at the woman, being careful not to show my fangs,

looked her in the eyes and said, " You are very welcome. We are

going to get you out of here now. But first I want you to listen to

what I have to say. You will not remember us being here or what

we have done. All you will remember is you woke up and found

the men dead. Do you understand?" She responded, "Yes." I

hated using the mind trick on her and the children. But it had to

be done so no one would learn what had happened that night or

about us. We arrived back at our house just before dawn. We had

carried the woman and children down the mountainside and left

them outside of the police station. The only thing they

remembered where the men who had taken them and were they

where held. It was a big thing on the news the next evening. But our existence was not revealed.

Chapter 17

THE WEDDING

Kim and Samuel's day had finally arrived! The ceremony was set for 8pm, right after dusk. All of the guests had arrived and were seated in our great hall. Since Kim had no family, we had deceived to have the wedding and reception after dark so all of our family and friends could attend. Since Mikel and Iris were still relatively new to the throne, they were to continue to reign until Samuel and Kim were ready to take over. The young couple wanted to travel and enjoy each others company before taking over the kingdom. Iris, Louisa and I were upstairs putting the finishing touches on the bride. Kim was absolutely beautiful! Her gown fit her body like a glove and her long red hair hung down her back in ringlets. Her veil was attached to the crown Camaz and I had given her. It was inlaid with diamonds and sapphires. The necklace she wore matched it perfectly.

When we had finished, I turned her to the mirror. She gasped

and said, "Is that really me!?" I replied, " Yes my dear, and no

one will be able to take their eyes off of you!" Camaz entered o

the room, dressed in his finest. I looked at him and smiled. God,

he was so handsome! He said, "Well, my dear, are you ready

to go marry the man you love?" Kim smiled at him and said,

"Yes sir, I am ready!" Camaz took Kim's hand and escorted her

from the room with Iris, Louisa and me right behind them.

The music was playing softly as we began our decent down the

long stairway. As we entered the Great Hall, everyone turned to

watch our approach. Samuel was standing at the alter and was

stunning in his black tuxedo, a blood red rose in the lapel.

When he saw his bride enter the room his whole face lit up with

the biggest smile I had ever seen. If I were still able to cry, I

would have been a total wreck. Kim and her uncle reached the

alter, he placed Kim's hand into Samuel's and the ceremony

began. The couple had written their own vows and spoke them with much emotion. Afterward Elder John then pronounced them man and wife. Samuel raised Kim's veil, and kissed her ever so tenderly.

Chapter 18

AWAITING THE HONEYMOONERS

After the reception Samuel and Kim left for their honeymoon.

Camaz and I went out hunting. We began searching for prey but

my head was not into the hunt. Camaz stopped me and asked, "

What is wrong, my love? To me, it seems like your heart is not

into the hunt tonight. Are you not thirsty?" I answered, " Yes, I

am very thirsty, but I cannot stop worrying about the kids. I am

still afraid they will do something stupid, like trying to have sex

before Kim is changed!" Camaz cupped my face in his hands

and said lovingly, "I understand your concern, dear heart, but

there is nothing we can do. We must have faith in the kids. I

spoke to Samuel, again, before they left and he assured me

nothing would happen. They are just going to be gone for a

week and he wanted her last week as a human to be her best." "I understand and that is all I want for her as well. But I remember

how I felt the night before you turned me. I wanted to make love

to you so badly that my whole body burned. At first I did not

think you felt the same, but now I know why you waited. I just

hope she does not talk him into it." "Love, Samuel is flesh of my

flesh and I know he has the self-control even if she does not.

Everything will be okay, you will see. So please stop worrying

and let us hunt, I am starving!" I giggled and said, " Alright, we

wouldn't want my king to die from starvation now would we?

Almost a week after the kids left for their honeymoon they

called to let us know everything was going well. They had been

calling every couple of days. We were in the process of

preparing for Kim's change. I could still remember the burning,

all those years ago. I hated that she would have to go through it.

I had spoken to Camaz and asked if there was something we

could give her to help with the pain, but unfortunately there wasn't. But I was right by her side to help her though it and to let her know how much she was loved. I knew she would ask me, over and over, to kill her, that was what I did with Camaz. But I would not kill her, just as he had not killed me. The kids were due back anytime. We had just woke from our long sleep and I was down in the chamber awaiting Kim so she could become as we are. Because Samuel was still very young he wasn't going to be making the change, Camaz would. I knew I could make the change as well, but I just couldn't bring myself to do it. Camaz called to me letting me know the kids had arrived and were on their way down. Kim entered the room, she looked so scared! I hugged her and told her everything would be alright. She said, " But I am so afraid, queen mother! " It will be alright Kim, I will be here with you the whole time. I know you are frightened but I promise it will not take long. You can hit, scratch and bite me as much as you want, you will not hurt me!"

Kim smiled at me and said, " You are so kind! I am so glad you are going to be my family!" Kim went to the bed we had prepared for her and laid down. Camaz went to her and explained what was going to happen and to not be afraid. He sat beside of her and she turned her head from him, exposing her neck. I was on the other side of her, holding her hand and talking to her. Camaz was like a snake and struck quickly and recoiled as quickly. He had explained to me, earlier, this is how a vampire is made. No blood is taken from the host and when the fangs were withdrawn the gene was passed on. So the burning was going to began soon. A little over one day into Kim's journey into our world I was still by her side. She had screamed for me to kill her so many times I had stopped counting! But I was there to comfort her. I kept telling her how wonderful her life would be and soon she would be with Samuel. Tears were streaming from her eyes and she said to me, in a tortured voice,

"Lady Anne, I love Samuel so much, I cannot wait for this to be over so I can be with him!" "And so you shall be child. You do not have much longer to wait! Have you noticed any change in the burning?" "Yes, my legs and arms feel cool now." " Good, that means you do not have much longer, child!" Late into the second day of Kim's transformation, most of the burning had left her body and was concentrated within her heart. I could hear her heart beating frantically, trying to escape the blistering fire, but that was a fight her heart would lose. I remembered right before my transformation was complete, how the scorching fire tried to rip my heart from my chest. All at once Kim's heart raced and thudded to a stop. She laid there so quite, then she opened her eyes. She looked up at all of us and smiled the most beautiful smile I had ever seen! Her delicate fangs glistened in the light. She was on her feet in a flash and had Samuel in her arms kissing him madly. She stepped back and said, " My god, this is so amazing! Why is my throat burning so badly?" Samuel

replied, " That is the thirst my dear, you will need to hunt!" So

off the two of them went to find Kim's first meal. Camaz and I

went on a hunting trip of our own. I was absolutely famished!

Chapter 19

THE GREAT BATTLE

Several years after Kim's transformation the kids settled in Mexico, with Mikel and Iris, at the royal palace. Camaz and I were still living and hunting in the mountains of North Carolina. It was so beautiful. I loved the home Camaz built for me. We were still as much in love as we were when I first met him. We had just arrived back home when there was a knock at the door. I opened the door and, to my surprise, it was Elder John. I invited him in and he asked where Camaz was. I told him Camaz was out back and asked what was wrong. He replied, "I have some very troubling news for the both of you." Camaz walked into the room and said, "My good friend John, what brings you to our home?" "Sire, I have come to let you both know there is a coup brewing back home. Several of the Elders are not happy with the way Mikel and Iris are ruling the country!" We both stared at John for a moment and then said at the same time, "Are you kidding? Are they crazy? They are both doing a wonderful job!!" John's response was, "I agree, but there are a few that do not! We need you to come back and settle this problem. I fear for the king and queen. There have been death threats made against them!" Camaz answered in shock, "What? How dare they threaten the king and queen! Who is behind this?" "We are not sure as they have been very secretive about this. It is why I was sent to have you come back!" "Then we must make ready to leave. Is the jet ready and waiting for us?" "Yes sire, it is." "Then let us waste no more time talking!" We rushed to get back to Mexico and to stop the uprising! We arrived at the castle a little after 9pm and were quickly greeted by our family. Mikel let us know everything that had been happening and the preparations being made. From the intel our elite guard had gathered, we knew an army was being amassed by a very old vampire named of Eric. He was originally from the old country and from what we were told, he was over 2000 years old. He wanted our kingdom for himself. He had seen how well our country was prospering and how very well stocked we were with the worst of the worst of human kind. Mikel said the council and elders where awaiting us in chambers. Camaz was over 900 years old, but this vampire was more than twice his age. He, too, was a born, not made, vampire. I was so frightened for my family and our beloved kingdom! We met with the council and elders, going over every detail of everything that had been discovered about Eric. He was a Viking vampire King and had ruled his lands for thousands of years. He was a fierce and ruthless tyrant who would stop at nothing to get what he wanted. Camaz told us his father had told him many stories of this horrible vampire and he was not to be taken lightly. Dawn was quickly approaching and we were making ready for our

sleep of death. All of our daylight protectors had been gathered

with Dempie in charge. I knew we would be safe with the

fairies, werewolves and demons we had to protect us during the

day. For this monster of a vampire must sleep as we do. But the

night would bring our greatest battle! That evening we were

awakened from our sleep to the sound of yelling. It was Dempie,

he was yelling that Eric's army was approaching the entrance to

our cavern. We leaped from our bed and made ready for the

battle. Camaz had asked me to stay in our chambers until he had

assessed the situation. I told him I did not want to leave his side,

but he insisted. So I was left to worry. Iris, Kristen, Kim and my

best friend, Louisa were lead into our chambers to await the

outcome. We were all fierce fighters in our own rights, but our

men did not want us in harms way. After an hour, Dempie

knocked on the door and announced himself so we would open

the door. I raced to the door and opened it asking, "Dempie, where is Camaz, Mikel and Samuel?" He replied, "They are still in battle, my lady, but Camaz has been wounded. We have taken him below for his protection. He sent me to bring you to him." If my heart could still beat it would have been racing! I told the other women to stay put and to not leave my chambers for any reason. I raced to be by my beloved's side. We entered the chamber where they had hidden Camaz and I rushed to his side. I looked down at my beloved husband and gasped. He had a large gash in his chest where a sword had sliced him and he was losing blood! I was horrified! He looked up at me and said, "My love, my life, please do not worry. It is a bad wound, but it will heal in time." "Oh Camaz, I do not know what I will do if you leave me! I will not be able to go on with out you! You are my life, my love, my heart!" Camaz reached for my hand and kissed it. He was so weak from the blood loss he was going in and out of consciousness. I had to stop the bleeding and find

someone for him to feed upon. I had been taught the healing

rights by my friend Louisa, so I knew what I had to do. I bit into

my wrist and opened a vain, placing my bleeding wrist over his

wound. As my blood flowed into his wound it began to close,

for you see, our blood had healing properties when used on

another vampire. Very few were aware of this practice. Finally

his wound sealed. I had to go to the holding cells and find the

worst of the worst for my dear husband to feed on. For my

protection Dempie accompanied me to the holding cells. While

we were below, Astor came to give us news of the battle. He

stated Eric had retreated, for the time being, but he felt it would

not be long before he tried to charge us again. We hurried to

make Camaz well, as he was the one who had to take on Eric.

As I looked down at my wounded husband, suddenly, a fire

began to build inside me. I had never felt such a fire, even during my change the fire was not as hot. I began to see red.

That horrible monster had done this to my beloved husband! He

was going to pay dearly! As I rose from beside Camaz, he

grabbed my hand and asked, "Where are you going, my love?

Why do you leave me?" I looked down at Camaz, he gasped and

said, "What is wrong with your beautiful blue eyes? They are

burning bright red!" I removed my hand from his and said, "I

have something I must do, but I promise you I will return to

you!" I quickly left the room. I returned to our chambers and

began putting on my weapons. I placed my sword in it's sheath

behind my back and my daggers on my arms and quickly left

the room. Within seconds, I was outside and running, at top

speed, across the battlefield. Everything in my vision was

burning red with hatred. When I reached the middle of the battle

I unsheathed my sword and took out anyone in my way. Finally

I reached the area where Eric was. He was standing over the

body of Sinclair. He was one of Mikel's closest friends. I leapt at Eric, welding my sword and landed in front of him. I swung but missed as he had sidestepped my attack. All the while, he was laughing. He said, "So, the king has sent a woman to do his dirty work! What a joke!" I looked at him with my blazing red eyes and he began to back away saying, "What is wrong with your eyes?" I replied, "This is what a mother and grandmother looks like when her family is threatened!" I lunged at him with my sword again and caught him across the chest. He backed away from me in disbelief. I sprung at him and landed squarely in the chest, knocking him to the ground. I removed one of my daggers and plunged it into his heart. He slowly began to die. I raised my sword, high above my head, and with one swift blow I removed his head from his shoulders.

Chapter 20

TRANSYLVANIA KING, THE TRUE DRACULA

One evening while Camaz and I were hunting, we heard the rapid approach of someone running. We knew it was a vampire as humans couldn't run that fast. We dropped into our protective stance readying for an attack. I reached behind my back for my sword. Suddenly Camaz stood up, grabbed my hand from behind my back and said, "It is okay, dear heart, I know who this vampire is. He is a messenger from my dear friend, the king of Transylvania." I looked up at Camaz and said, "You have never spoke of being friends with him. How long have you known him?" "My dear, I have known him my entire UN-dead life. He is my godfather." Wow, I thought to myself and Then asked, "Please tell me his name is not Dracula!" and giggled. Camaz looked down at me, smiled and said, "No, my dear, his name is not Dracula, but the stories are based on him. His name is Bodgan and he is the leader of the order of the Dracul." The man approached us and said, "Sire, it is good to see you again!" "It is good to see you as well Stephen. May I introduce my wife, the Lady Anne?" Stephen smiled at me and said, " It is a great honor to meet you, my Lady!" I smiled at him and said, " Thank you. I am very pleased to meet you as well!" Stephen told Camaz he had much to speak with him about so we headed back to our home. When we woke the next evening, Camaz told me all he had learned from Stephen. I was shocked to hear what he told me. King Bodgan was having problems with an outcast he had sent away many years before. He was one of the Kings closest friends and a knight in the Order of the Dragon, or Dracul if you used the proper word. This knight had done terrible things to the countryside villages, taking the lives of the innocent. So Bodgan banished him from his lands. But he had returned, several months prior and was trying to take the throne.

He had amassed a huge army and Bodgan was in need of our help. Two days later we arrived in Transylvania. We went to speak to Bodgan right away. He had found as many werewolves as was possible and quite a few fairies and demons as well. Camaz told him not to worry, we would be right there, by his side, helping in the battle. Bodgan asked if we would like to see his beautiful countryside and go hunting. I agreed quickly as I was very thirsty! We went into the beautiful night, hunting for our next meal. The countryside of Transylvania was quite stunning and the aroma of the flora and fauna was intoxicating! Bodgan had told us there had been reports of some very bad men killing villagers in nearby Abtsdorf. He also told us his people were very loyal to him and reported to him any time there was a problem. The men had already killed twenty villagers and it was time they paid with their lives! We had been running for about twenty minutes when we came upon a clearing in the woods. I sniffed the air and there it was! The

wonderful smell of evil! I looked at Camaz and Bodgan, pointed

and dropped into my hunting crouch. There were three men

huddled around a campfire making what looked like their

dinner. Little did they know they were on the menu! I told the

guys to wait and let me approach the campfire first, so I could

have a little fun before we killed them. I slowly walked into

their campsite and asked, "Hello. I have gotten lost can any of

you gentlemen give me directions back to town?" They all

looked at each other and one of them said, "Sure, little lady, we

would love to help you!" Then he lunged at me. I side-stepped

him, making him fall, face first, to the ground. The other two

men charged me and I leaped straight up and hovered in midair.

They all looked up at me and said, "Vampire" in Romanian.

They ran toward the woods and straight into Camaz and

Bodgan's waiting arms. I was by their side in no time and had the third man pinned to the ground. He fought me, but it was of no use. I was a 100 times stronger than he. I pushed his head to the side and struck. His blood was warm and delicious. I drank him slowly, savoring every drop until I had drained him dry. I rolled off him and laid there for a moment, enjoying my full belly. Camaz walked up to me and asked, "Did you enjoy your meal, my dear?" I looked lovingly at him and replied, "Oh my yes! That was one of the best meals I have ever had!" Camaz laughed heartily and asked, "Are you ready to go back to the castle? We have much war planning to do!" I answered, "Yes." He placed my hand in his and we ran back to the castle.

Chapter 21

READYING FOR WAR

When we arrived at the castle, Bodgan took us to the Great

War Room so we could begin planning our defense against

Alexandru, who had once been Bodgan's closest friend. Bodgan

had been informed Alexandru's army had reached the port

city of Constanta. They were beginning to move inland toward

the castle. It was a 4 day ride so we had very little time to plan.

In the war room were many of Bodgan's top advisers and

warriors. As with Camaz, Bodgan's right hand man was a fairy

and was as fierce as our own Dempie. His name was Virgiliu.

After introductions were made, we all settled down at the war

table and began work on our plans. The castle had already been

manned with extra werewolves, fairies and demons for daytime

protection. We also were ready for anything attacking by night.

As Camaz and I made ready for our sleep of death I asked him,

"Darling, I do not want to sound worried, but I am. Do you think we will be safe during the day?" Camaz laid down beside me and touched his hand to my face."You have nothing to fear my darling, there are plenty of guards to protect us. Even if they do make it to our chambers I would protect you with my life!" I rolled to face him and smiled. I ran my hand down his stone hard chest, still marveling at it's smoothness. I continued downward until I reach his manhood and gently stroked it. In an instant he was on top of me, kissing me wildly. I felt him enter me and I screamed into his mouth. God I loved this man!! The following evening, when we woke, we learned the enemy army was only a day's ride from the castle. It was was jumping with activity. We met with Bodgan in the war room. He had received word from his scouts that there were over 1000 werewolves, fairies, demons. Also over 2000 vampires headed our way. Some of the vampires were very old and had well honed fighting skills. But many of the army were very young, so we had that to our advantage as most of our vampires are very old. We knew the enemy would send in the younger ones first, we arranged for our best warriors to be on the front lines. They would be able to take out the young ones quickly. We would then deal with the older ones. All we could do at that point was wait. Camaz and I decided to go hunting outside of the castle so we would be ready for battle the following evening. Bodgan had the dungeons well stocked as well, so we would not run out of food. It was not always necessary to completely drain our victims, sometimes we take only enough to get us by. Oh, but do I love draining them, watching the life leave their eyes! As we were hunting, I picked up a whiff of something delicious. I stopped and tested the air to determine the direction that the wonderful smell was coming from and caught it to the left of me. I pointed in the direction for Camaz and dropped into my hunting crouch with him following close behind me. We entered a small clearing with a cabin. Smoke was billowing from the chimney so we knew someone was home. The distinct smell

told us there were two men inside who had done very terrible

things. I went to the front of the cabin and Camaz to the back,

so there would be on escape. I walked to the door and knocked.

A tall, slender man answered the door and asked, "How may I

help you, little lady?" I looked up at him with my most

seductive stare and replied, "Hello there, I seem to have lost my

way. Do you have a phone I can use?" I saw the lust building in

his eyes as he said, "Sure, come on in. I will take you to it." I

entered the house and followed the man to the kitchen. There, at

the table, sat the other man. He was huge and looked very

powerful. But he was no match for me. With but a thought, I

summoned Camaz and he was quickly in the house. The men

shouted in unison, "What the hell!" At the moment my body

collided into the bigger man, knocking him from his chair to the

floor, Camaz had the other man pinned to the floor. We both

struck at the same time. My meal was fighting me with all of his strength but it was like a kitten fighting a rattlesnake. I sank my fangs deep into his jugular and began to drink. After a few minutes he went limp. I could hear his heart slowing and then it stopped. I rose up off of him and wiped the blood from my mouth. Camaz had completely drained his victim as well and was ready to go back to the castle. Soon it would be daylight. The battle would begin as evening approached. We returned to the castle to sleep so we would be well rested.

Chapter 22

BATTLE CRIES

We woke the following evening to the sounds of shouting from above. We were under attack. We sprang from our bed and dressed in our battle gear. I pulled my hair up into a ponytail so it would not interfere with reaching my sword. I placed my knives in their sleeves and was ready to fight. We rushed upstairs to find everyone preparing to fight. The enemy army was right outside the castle walls, trying to make their way in. Camaz and I took our places beside Bodgan and readied for battle. There was a great crashing sound coming from the castle entrance. Someone shouted, "Battering ram! They have crashed the castle doors!" I reached behind me and unsheathed my sword making ready for the attack. Camaz and Bodgan had made ready as well. The next thing I knew, there was werewolves, demons and fairies everywhere. They all rushed at

us at once. A fairy charged at me with his sword drawn. I leaped
into the air just as he was about to strike me. I swung my sword
downward and removed his head. His body fell to the ground
and blood poured from his neck. I landed and kicked his head
against the wall. I ran to join the others. Camaz was in a fierce
battle with another vampire, he looked to be very old. Later I
would learn the vampire was over 2000 years old. He had a
very old world look to him. He was fighting fiercely with
Camaz, he swung his sword and cut Camaz across the chest,
causing a gaping wound. Camaz fell to the ground. I screamed
and ran toward the vampire. He was about to take Camaz's
head. I leaped into the air and landed on his back, jarring him
backwards away from Camaz. Our battle began. He was very
strong and was tried to subdue me, but I had become a very
skilled fighter over the years. I broke free of him and jumped
straight up into the air. But before I knew it, he had done the
same. We were suspended in midair. He spoke, "You are no

match for me, little one! I have been on this earth for many years. I have defeated your husband and he is much older then you! So prepare to die!" At that moment he lunged toward me, with sword blazing. I laughed and dropped to the ground, causing him to miss me completely. He screamed and dropped down after me. I turned swinging my sword with all my might. The blade struck his neck and his head dropped to the ground. I ran over to where Camaz was laying and looked at him. He had a large gash in his beautiful chest. The blood was leaving him quickly. I needed to close the wound or he would die. I picked him up and ran to our room in the lower quarters and laid him on our bed. I bit into my wrist and poured the flowing blood over his wound. I knew this would stop the bleeding but I did not know how much blood he had lost. He was very weak. He stared up at me, smiled and said, "My warrior queen, you are my heart, my love, my life! I swore to protect you with my life but it was you who saved me!" I smiled at him, bent down and kissed him on his trembling lips. " I told you if it came down to it I would protect you with my life as well and I have kept my promise, my one true love!" The wound had begun to close but he was still very weak. I needed to get more of my blood into him or he would die. I turned my head and exposed my neck to him saying, "Drink, my love." He turned his head toward my neck and gently bit me. I could feel my blood flowing into his mouth as he drank. I could feel him getting stronger with each mouthful. He reached for me, putting his arms around me, gently rocking me back and forth in his arms. He released his hold on my neck and kissed me ever so gently. I could taste my blood in his mouth. We released our hold on one another and Camaz said, "I am feeling much better, my love. We need to get back to the battle." We were off again, hopefully not into a massacre. We arrived to a scene of madness. There were bodies everywhere and still many more fighting. We searched for Bodgan and found him battling a demon. Another vampire entered the room where the battle was happening. He was a

large, muscular man with tattoos on both arms. They were

dragons. I knew at once, who this vampire was. It was

Bodgan's former best friend, Marcus. He yelled Bodgan's name

and rushed towards him with a sword in each hand. I yelled,

"Look out!" as I raced across the room toward the two men. I

leaped onto Marcus' back and sunk my daggers into his neck,

but he just tossed me, like a rag doll, into the wall. I hit with

such force I was momentarily stunned. I watched, in disbelief,

as my husband charged Marcus. I had never seen Camaz move

that fast before. He was like a blur and then he was attacking

Marcus. They were moving so fast it was hard to see them,

even for my vampire eyes. All of a sudden they stopped. Camaz

was on top of Marcus with a sword at his throat. With one quick

slice he removed Marcus' head. Camaz rushed to me and asked,

" My dear, are you okay?" I looked up at him and replied, "I

think so. I hit the wall pretty hard, so I'm just now getting my senses back." Camaz reached down and gently lifted me to my feet. I was still a little unsteady so he put his arm around my waist. We went to where Bodgan was laying. He had some nasty wounds but they were not life threatening. Once Marcus was destroyed, the rest of his army fled. We lost many good fighters that day, including Dempie! I still miss him the most. Camaz was very saddened by the loss of one of his best friends. We took his body back to Mexico after Bodgan had recovered. Dempie's clansmen had been alerted of his death and were making preparations for his burial. Three weeks after the battle Bodgan was completely recovered and ready, once again, to take full control of his kingdom. We said our goodbyes as we would be flying out in a few hours to take Dempie home. I had grown to love this country and it's people. I would miss it but it was time to go home.

Chapter 23

FAREWELL TO A GOOD FRIEND

We arrived at the airport around 9pm and we were greeted by Dempie's family and friends. It was a sad day for all of us. While we were waiting for his coffin to be unloaded from the plane we were introduced to Dempie's parents. His mother, Elaina, was stunning with long black hair flowing down her back. His father, Marco, was very handsome and distinguish. They had invited us back to their place so we left the airport and head up into the mountains. Some time later we arrived at the fairies encampment. There were small houses with neatly groomed lawns scattered around the countryside. We drove a few more minutes and arrived at our host's house. It was a two story home with many beautiful flowers and plants. I told Elaina what a beautiful home she had, she smiled at me and said, "Thank you." I still had trouble adjusting to the fairies' smile.

Their teeth are very sharp and plentiful! We entered the house and I was amazed at how beautiful the furnishings were. Elaina told me they traveled all over the world looking for unique pieces. The men went to the pouch, out back, to talk about Dempie. Elaina took me up to the second floor and showed me to our room saying, "I hope these accommodations will suit you your Highness." I smiled at her and said, "No need for formalities just call me Anne." She responded, "As you wish". She asked me if I would like to see Dempie's room, there were many treasures in there. I told her I just couldn't right then. It was still to soon and his death had taken a toll on me. I could imagine what Camaz was feeling right then. It was getting late and we had yet to hunt. I was becoming very thirsty, so I thanked Elaina and returned downstairs. Camaz was waiting for me in the living-room. He smiled at me and said, "I know that look my dear, you are very hungry!" I answered, "Yes Camaz, that I am. Shall we hunt?" "I too have become very thirsty so yes, let's hunt". We left Dempie's parent's home and went down the mountainside to villages below. It was a little after 1am so there was very few people out and about. Camaz alerted me he had picked up on a scent so we began searching for out next meal. We were in the heart of the city the scent had became very strong. We dropped down into our hunting crouch and began stalking the wonderful scent. Soon we came upon two men in a alleyway, they had a woman pinned down and were attempting to rape her. I told Camaz to stay behind for a few minutes as I wanted to play with our food first. He laughed and said, "My dear you never cease to amaze me!" So I left Camaz's side and began walking toward the alleyway. The woman was fighting wildly for her life, she was battered and bloody. The two men were taking turns with her. I walked up behind them and said, "Hey, why don't you pick on someone your own size!" They mumbled something in Spanish, then one of the men ran at me. He grabbed me and I let him tackle me to the ground. He began tearing at my clothing and I began to laugh. He screamed at me to stop laughing or he would shut me up. I looked up at him and said, "Tonight it will be I who will be shutting you up for good!" He looked at me in disbelief and replied, "So just how are you going to to that?!" I replied, " This is how!" I smashed my fist into his mouth knocking out about four teeth. He screamed in pain. But the smell of his blood had taken over me. I slammed his bloody face to the side and struck. He was fighting for his life, but it was of no use! In the mean time Camaz had the other man down on the ground and was draining him. The woman was unconscious and unaware of what was taking place. I pulled in the last drop of his sweet blood and jumped to my feet. I told Camaz I was going to take the woman to the nearest hospital for help. I would leave her somewhere she could be found. So off we went to try and save the woman's life. We dropped the woman off at the hospital and we had to hurry, it was getting close to daylight. We arrived back at our fairy friends house just in time. We hurried up to our room.

Elainia had already made our room sun proof so we would be

able to rest peacefully. We took off our soiled clothing and we

got into the shower together. Camaz loved to wash my body and

I enjoyed every minute of it. Once we were both clean and dry

we laid down in the bed and began our sleep of death. The next

evening when we awoke and went downstairs. There were many

fairies in the living room. They were the closest friends and

family of our dear Dempie. There was much sadness in the

room. We learned his viewing would be held at 8pm and then

we would go to the grave site. It was explained that fairies were

not put in a box and buried but instead they were laid to rest in

the ground naturally, for mother earth to reclaim them. The

viewing and burial was done very nicely. There was many in

attendance from all across the supernatural world. Dempie had

many werewolves, vampires and demons as friends. He was

loved by every one. So, as we said our last goodbyes to our dear friend. I thought back to when I first met him. He was such a

charmer! He was surely missed!

Chapter 24

A TIME OF RECKONING

We had been back home for a little over a year since the great battle that took a lot of our friends from us. They were all dearly missed, but Dempie we missed the most! Camaz had been called out of town on vampire business and I had stayed behind. This was the first time in many years we had been separated. I had stayed behind because the kids had come for a visit and had been there since before Camaz left. Samuel was getting ready to take over his role as our next king. Camaz had gone to the counsel to finalize everything. Kim was very nervous about becoming the queen, but I put her mind at ease letting her know that they would be very well protected. Camaz and I had discussed moving back to Mexico so we could be with all of our family and friends. We had agreed we would be returning for good when Samuel was crowned the king. I loved living in the North Carolina mountains, but I missed all of my family in Mexico. My parents had passed away a few years ago and my brothers were both married with families. They had no idea that I was still around, as they think I died many years ago. In a way they were right, I did die, but I came back this wondrous creature. I never looked back when I allowed Camaz to take me. I loved the night and the night loved me! We arrived in the mountains of Mexico three days later and met up with our men. I was so happy to see Camaz! It had been over a week since he left and I had been yearning to be in his arms again! I ran up to him and jumped into his arms. He hugged me tenderly and said, "My love, my life, I have missed you!" "As I have missed you as well!" He kissed me gently and said, "We have much to discuss, shall we retire to our quarters?" I looked up at him and smiled saying, "Your wish is my command my king!" We said out goodbyes to everyone and went down to our chambers. Once we were behind closed doors, Camaz gabbed me and started tearing my clothes from my body. His hands ran

up and down my body as he passionately kissed me. He

whispered into my mouth, "I need you my queen! I need to

feel myself inside of you now!" I wiggled closer to him and

pressed my naked body against his and said, "You have no idea

how I have waited to hear you say that! Take me my king!"

Camaz throw me onto the bed and began stroking my breast. He

sent tiny shivers of pleasure down my spine. He began kissing

down my neck, for he knew it was my weakness! It drove me

wild with need! I pulled him back up to my lips and kissed him

madly. We made love for hours that night. Like it was our first

time! I reminded him later to never leave me again! The next

evening we awoke to a great disturbance. We dressed quickly

and headed upstairs to see what was going on. Samuel and Kim

were in a heated debate about them becoming the next king and

queen. Mikel and Iris were there with them. We went up to them

and asked what was going on. Samuel replied, "Kim does not

want me to take the throne. She thinks it is to dangerous. I tried to explain to her that everything would be alright but she is so frightened." I went over to Kim and said, "My dear, I felt the same way when Camaz told me about becoming the queen and ruling our country. I was still very young, younger than you where, when I was made vampire. So I know what the fear can entail. Camaz and I have been through many battles during and after we where king and queen so you have nothing to fear." She looked at me and I could see the fear in her eyes. I told her, "You know, when I was first made vampire, I knew nothing of fighting. I was taught everything I know from some wonderful friends and family. You will learn all that you will need to survive as I will train you myself!" Kim smiled at me and said, "Oh, lady Anne, I am so glad you are going to train me. I have watched you fight and you are amazing!" I smiled back at her and said, "Good, so tomorrow we will start your training. Now I don't know about you but I am starving! Shall we hunt?"She replied, "Oh yes, I am famished!" So off we all went to find our

next meal. Samuel and Kim came with us. So while we where

hunting I continued to try and comfort Kim. She had become

quite a skilled huntress! I watched as she scented the air and

caught that wonderful smell. She looked back at us with a great

spark in her eyes and said, "Do you smell that! So delicious! I

have scented at least three, possibly more." So we all dropped

down into our hunting crouch and let Kim take the lead. She had

taken us deep into the heart of the city. Where all of the poor and

hopeless lived. We came upon a large house in a very run down

neighborhood and she pointed to the house and said, "There,

that is where the scent is coming from!" We all surrounded the

house, each of us checking for our prey. I suddenly heard

screaming coming from inside the house. But it was very faint,

the person was gagged. But I had no trouble hearing her pleas

with my strong ears. I have pinpointed her exact location and

opened a window, slipping in. I could hear the others entering the house from different points. Once inside I headed to the area where I heard the screams. I entered the room and in the middle there was a woman bound and gagged. She had no clothes on and was bruised and battered. She looked up at me and I put a finger to my lips so she would know to be quite. I scanned the room for my prey and discovered him in a adjoining bathroom taking a shower. I whispered to the woman not to worry, I would be back then slipped from the room into the bathroom. The man was having himself a good old time singing in the shower. I was going to have some fun! I removed my clothing, slide back the shower curtain and joined him in the shower. The look on his face was first one of shock and then I watched as the lust begun to build in his eyes and body. The man reached over and stroked my face and said, "My god you are beautiful! Who are you? An angel sent from heaven?" I looked up at him, smiling so that I bared my fangs for him to see and replied, " My dear man, I am far from being an angel, what I am, is your worst nightmare!" At that point he began to scream. I punched him in the mouth and knocked all of his teeth out. The blood began to run down his face. At that point the fun was over. My thirst took over and I attacked him. When I had finished there was not a drop of blood to be found anywhere. I even licked the blood from is face! I left his lifeless body in the shower, cleaned myself off so not to scare the woman and returned to release her. I untied her and removed her gag. She was very weak, she had been raped many times and was dehydrated. I helped her up from the floor and she asked, "Who are you? The police?" I replied, "No my dear, I am just someone who heard your screams and wanted to help. Do not worry about the man or any of the others, they have also been taken care of!" She replied, "Good, I hope they all suffered!" "Oh, believe me, they did!" She laughed at my remark and we headed downstairs to join up with the others. There are two other women with the others. They looked like they had been to hell and back. I went up to

Camaz and asked, "Did we get them all?" He replied, "Yes my dear, there was six in all including yours, they will not be harming anyone ever again!" I thought to myself, "Good!" I told the woman I saved she needed to call the police and tell them where to find them. I handed her my victim's phone and we all left. We had great fun, but I was ready to get back home and into my beloved's arms! The next evening I spoke with Kim and began her training in all arts of fighting. She was so happy I was helping her. She was going to make a wonderful queen!

Chapter 26

THE CROWNING OF THE KING AND QUEEN

The following year we where making ready for the carnation of

Samuel and Kim. With my training and help from others she

had become a skilled fighter and I knew she would be able to

defend herself and Samuel if need be. But I would always be

there for her if she needed me. One day while we were talking

she asked me about Camaz and my crowning. I explained to her

we were married and crowned on the same day. She asked me

what my dress had looked like. I told her to hold on and went to

my closet to retrieve my dress. I showed it to her and she fell in

love with it. She asked me if it were possible for her to wear it

for her coronation. I told her I would be honored if she wore it.

I also gave her my crown, necklace and bracelets to wear. We

had to do little alterations to the dress, as it fit her almost to a

tee! That evening while Camaz and I where out hunting I told him about my dress and how stunning she looked in it. He

smiled at me and said, "My dear, Kim is quite lovely, but no

woman can hold a torch to your beauty!" I looked up at him,

smiled and said, "Darling, you know, flattery will get you

everywhere with me!" He laughed and picked me up, encircling

me in his arms and kissed me passionately. We made love under

the moon and stars. A few hours later he asked me if I was

ready to hunt, that our love making had made him very thirsty. I

gave him my most seductive smile and said, "And I thought you

only hungered for my body!" He laughed and said, "Woman,

one of these days, you are going to be the death of me!" But

Camaz was right, the thirst had taken over me as well. So off

we went in search of that wonderful smell. Later that evening

we arrived back at the castle and everyone was readying for the

sleep of death. The next night would be Samuel and Kim's big

day. Mikel and Iris would be handing over the throne to them.

So we all needed to get rested for the event. The next day was the big day! There had been much going on in the castle as we made ready for our new King and Queen. Mikel and Iris had decided to leave here for awhile. They wanted to go off and explore the world. Samuel and Kim had decided after they had been king and queen for a year they would start searching for a surrogate to bear Samuel's children. I had a long talk with Kim a few years back and explained the process that Camaz and I had to go through to have children. She completely understood and was all for keeping the line going. But I knew when the time came she would need my support because of the jealousy! We had all now gathered in the great hall awaiting Samuel, Kim, Mikel and Iris. Just then Samuel entered the hall totally out of his mind! He was yelling that someone had taken Kim and he couldn't find her anywhere! Camaz and I sprung into action, telling everyone to start searching the castle and grounds. I had became very close to Kim and had been able to pick up her thoughts every now and then. At first I thought I was going crazy, but Camaz told me sometimes it happened when you became very close to someone. I had to go somewhere very quite and open up my mind to her. I told Camaz I was going up the the top of the castle and to not let anyone disturb me. I sat on the ledge, closed my eyes and opened my mind. I was very good at it with Camaz, but I had never tried with anyone else. I sat very still and listened with my mind. At first nothing, but then I picked up a very faint whisper. It was calling to me. I concentrate harder and then I heard her. She was crying out in her mind for Samuel. I begun to talk to her in my mind, letting her know that I was there with her and we would find her. Then I heard her say, "Lady Anne is that you?" I replied, " Yes, my dear, it is I, can you tell me anything about your abductors?" Then I heard her say, "All I can tell you is they are not vampires. I have never come across a creature that looks like them." "Can you describe what they look like?" "Yes, they are very tall and thin. They have greenish skin and pointed ears. Their mouths are full of razor sharp

teeth." I thought to myself for a moment and then asked, "Kim

have you ever meet a ghoul?" "No, I don't think so, why?"

"Because that is what you just described. Do not worry we are

coming for you. We know where the ghouls live!" Kim then

said in a weak voice, "Please hurry." I ran back down to where

the others where at and let them know what I had found out. We

had never had a good relationship with the ghouls and they had

been trying to start a war with us for years. But we did have

some very close friends that were ghouls, so we went to meet

with them. Our two friends were named Otto and Damon. We

gave them all of the information I had learned from Kim and we

made our rescue plans. Otto and Damon had friends inside of

the ghoul's lands and had gotten word to them to be ready for

our arrival. The ghouls lived under a large cemetery outside of

town. They were nothing more than viscous animals, with the

exception of a few. When we arrived at the graveyard, Otto and

Damon showed us the entrance to their lair. We began our journey down into the depths of their home. Our two friends told us it had been many years since they had left their home. They where not happy with the way things where there. Camaz had met them about seventy-five years ago and had brought them under his wing. They had become very close. We reached the bottom and Otto held up his hand to stop us. He signaled to his brother that there are many waiting for us. Damon whispered to us to let us know to be ready for battle. I drew my sword from my back and made ready for the attack. We rushed the room, there was so many of them down there, it was unbelievable! We were out number, but we were fierce fighters so we charged at the group. All of a sudden someone from the other side yelled, "STOP or the girl dies!" We stopped for a moment and the ghouls parted waves. We spotted the ghoul that had commanded us to stop. He was very old and looked to be their king. Kim was strapped down to what looked like an alter.

He was standing above her with a wicked looking sword. He said, " If you come any closer I will remove her head from her body!" Camaz had to restrain Samuel as he was ready to charge at the ghoul. I spoke up and asked, "Why have you taken this woman? She has done nothing to you!" He looked at me and laughed saying, "No she has done nothing to me but your husband has! He has taken all that is dear to me, my loving wife and son. I knew I could not get close enough to you, so I took the next best thing! So now, if you do not wish for the girl to die, then come and take her place!" Camaz screamed at the ghoul, "No! Never! You will not touch my wife!!" "Then the girl will die!" He swung back the blade and readied himself to kill Kim. I yelled at him, "Stop! I will come with you, please release her!" Camaz grabbed my arm and said, "No, I will not let you! You are my life. I am nothing with out you!" I looked up at him, smiled and said, " I know my love, but I cannot allow Kim to die. I have lived a long and very happy life with you, but they have only just began theirs. I'm sorry my love but I must do this." I removed his hand from my arm and began walking toward the ghoul,where Kim was at. Once I reached the alter he released Kim. She grabbed and hugged me saying, "Why are you doing this? Are you crazy! He will kill you!" I stepped back and said, "I know you do not understand this now but you will in the future. I am willing to lay down my life for anyone in my family, including you! Now go to Samuel and get out of here!" Kim kissed me on my cheek and said, "I love you!" Then she ran to Samuel. I turned and looked at my beloved and said, "I am sorry Camaz, but it had to be done, they are the future of our race. I love you!" I then turned back to the ghoul. He grabbed and tied me down to the alter. Then said, "Now vampire king, watch your queen die, as I watched my family die!" I was screaming over an over in my head, "Camaz I love you, you are my live, my love, please take care of our children!" I closed my eyes and awaited for my final breath. I heard the swoosh of the sword's blade as he swung. I thought

back to all of the happy times I had with Camaz, I knew he

would miss me, but he must go on. Then I feel the cold steel of

the blade as it touched my neck, then nothing but darkness. I

thought, "Where am I? I feel like I am floating! But there is

nothing but blackness all around me. Have I died and gone to

hell? No wait, hell is very hot and very bright from everything I

have ever read. Not total darkness. I could hear many voices

around me but I couldn't see anyone. Had my long passed

family come to get me? Would I see my mother and father? I

wished I could see my beloved one more time. I already missed

him so much. The voices around me sounded like they were in a

tunnel, I had heard that when you die there was a tunnel where

your loved ones would be waiting on you. But these voices did

not sound like my human family, they sound like my vampire

family! Has the ghouls killed them all as well! Please, please

someone wake from this nightmare!" Just then I felt the cool lips of someone kissing my cheek and then I heard Camaz! I

think, "Oh god, he is dead to! The ghouls have killed him to!"

Then I heard his sweet voice whispering to me, "Baby, please,

please, come back to me! I am here by your side and you are

safe!" All of a sudden I thought, "I'm not dead? He is alive and

I am alive? So why am I in this darkness?" I then remembered

something that Camaz had told me a long time ago. When a

vampire received a mortal wound sometimes they can heal

themselves from within and there was stories of a great

darkness while the healing process was going on. But then I

thought, "I felt the blade on my throat, he had to have removed

my head. No vampire could come back from that!" So I

pondered all of that information for a while. I could still hear

Camaz calling my name and asking me to wake up. But how

could I wake up, I'm dead. So I pondered some more. Then

something began to change, my body did not feel as light as

before, it felt like I was floating downward toward the ground and then all of a sudden I was inside my body. I could feel all of

my senses come alive. I opened my eyes and looked up to the

face of an angel, my beloved Camaz! I said in a weak voice,

"Camaz, what happened to me?" He replied, "I thought I could

get to you in time, but the monster cut your throat deeply. But

he did not take your head. I stopped the blade from going any

farther. I took the sword from him and killed him. We brought

you back here and I bled into your wound and gave you my

blood to drink. I thought I had lost you, it took so long for you

to come back to me!" "How long was I out?" Camaz replied,

"My dear you left me for a little more that a year! I thought I

would never get you back!!" "A year, are you kidding! It took

me a year to heal?" "Yes my dear and I have never left your

side. I knew you would come back to me some day!" Camaz

bent down and kissed me gently on my lips, I breathed him in.

It was so good to be able to smell his scent again! I broke the

kiss and asked, "If you have not left my side for over a year, how have you feed?" "My dear, because of my age, I can go up to 6 months without feeding. So I have had the children bring me two men in the last year." I looked at him and said, "Wow!" Camaz laughed and said, "You need to rest now dear, you still have a long recovery ahead of you." I reached up to my neck and I felt the long gash there. I gasped, thinking, "Will I be scared from now on!" Camaz sensed my distress and said, "Do not worry yourself my dear, my blood is healing the scar. It will be gone soon." I think to myself, "I hope he is right, it feels horrible!" Then the darkness took me again. But I was not afraid for I knew it was only the healing process. Soon I would be in my loving Camaz's arms again!

Chapter 27

LOUISA'S STORY

During my recovery my best friend Louisa stayed at my side the whole time. While she was nursing me back to health we talked about her life. Louisa was only a few years younger than Camaz and had been through some really great adventures. Louisa was born in the year 1260 so that made her 750 years old. She had seen many things in her long life, including all of the major wars. She told me there had only been one great love in her life. His name was Christen. They met during the Mexican American war. She told me he was a major in the American army. They had met one night while he was out scouting the area. He had been very kind to her and offered to escort her home. Telling her that it was very dangerous for such a beautiful lady to be out so late at night. Louisa said from that moment she fell in love with him. They had met many nights after that and their love affair grew stronger with each passing

night. After about 2 weeks he told her he wanted to ask her

something. He asked, "Why can I only see you at night? I

would love to take you out and show you off during the day!

Are you married?" Louisa said she laughed when he ask her that

and responded. "No my dear man I am not married. There is

much that you do not know about me and would not believe if I

told you." Christen then responded, "Why would I not believe

you? I love you!" Louisa told me that was the first time he had

ever told her that he loved her. She then smiled at him letting

him see her delicate fangs. She said he jumped back from her

and asked about them. Louisa began to tell him about her life as

a vampire. At first he just starred at her in disbelief. But then

told her he believed her. She ask him if he was afraid, he just

laughed and said. "No I am not afraid of you, the only thing

I'm afraid of is losing you!" So that night she sealed their bond

in blood. Christen made a wonderful vampire and they spent

many years together. But about 100 year ago he met his tragic death in a great battle and she had been alone every since. This made me very sad. I had such a great loving husband and she was all alone. So I promised myself that some day I would find her someone that would love her as much as Camaz loved me! So my search for the perfect man or vampire began for my dearest friend. That evening while Camaz and I where hunting I told him of my plan to find someone for Louisa. He told me she had suffered deeply when Christen was killed and did not know if she could love again. He had been her one true love. He told me he would not take another if anything where to happen to me, I was his one true love. I was so overwhelmed by what he had said I leaped into his arms and began kissing him madly. We made love for hours that night like it was our first time! But I would still try and find someone who could make Louisa as happy as Camaz made me! I began my search in the vampire kingdoms, checking on all available royal males. I was very picky about who I wanted to meet my best friend and had

narrowed it down to ten, two kings and eight princes. I arranged

a great ball and invite all of them. I would let her meet them and

hopefully she would find her new love. A few weeks later it was

the day of the ball. As I was getting ready Louisa came into my

room. She looked stunning! Her gown was a pale purple with

pearls studding the top. Atop her head was a crown encrusted

with rubies and emeralds. I smiled at her and said, "Wow! You

look beautiful!" She smiled back at me and said, "Thank you. I

just came in to see if you needed any help getting ready." I

answered, " Sure, if you would like, can you just zip up my

dress." So while Louisa helped me finish getting ready we

talked for a bit. I told her I was sad because she did not have

anyone to love her and that was why I had arranged the ball. So

she could meet new people. She told me I didn't have to do that,

but she was grateful I had. I told her about the two kings and

eight princes I had invited and I had chosen them very carefully.

I only wanted the best for my best friend! We both were

giggling when Camaz came into our room. He looked at me

slyly and asked, "May I ask what you two are up to? I could

hear your giggles all the way down the hall!" I smiled at my

husband and said, " Just a private joke my dear, nothing for you

to concern yourself with!" So Camaz took my hand and we all

went down to the great hall for the party. There were over 200

in attendance and the party was well on the way. Camaz

excused himself for a moment while he went over to talk to

Dempie's parents. We had not seen them since we lost him

in the great battle. At just that moment a very handsome young

man came up to us and said, "Good evening ladies, my name is

Richard and who might I have the pleasure of meeting?" I

looked at Louisa and back to him and said, " I am very pleased

to meet you Richard, my name is Anne. I am the wife of Camaz

and this is his sister Louisa." He looked at us and said, " I am

very pleased to meet you both. Lady Louisa, would you care to dance?" Louisa smiled at him and said, "I would love to!" So off they went onto the dance floor. I thought to myself, "I hope he is the right one for her. She deserves to be happy." So that is how Louisa and Richard became a couple.

Chapter 28

A TIME OF GREAT JOY

It had been one year since Louisa and Richard met. They had

been together every since. Louisa had been spending most of

her time in Richard's kingdom, getting to know his family and

friends. I had just received notice from her they were to wed

in a month. So we were making plans to leave for England in a

few weeks. The children were staying behind to watch over the

kingdom. I was so excited to see my friend again! I had missed

her so! But Kim and myself had became quite good friends, so

that helped a little. I was so happy Louisa had found someone

to spend the rest of eternity with. But I would miss not having

her around to talk with anymore! Camaz and I were going

hunting that night. We had just received notice there was a man

killing women in town and he had already taken the lives of ten.

We had to find him and stop him before he could kill again. We took to the air and went in search of the madman. A few

minutes later we arrived in town and set down on top of one of

the buildings. We perched there on a ledge and let our sense of

smell take over, testing the air for our pray. Soon I picked up on

a faint hint of the wonderful aroma. I pointed to the east and

Camaz smiled. We took to the air again and began to search for

our next meal. Then I spotted him below in a dark alley. He had

a woman pinned against the wall with a knife at her throat. He

had already cut her once because the sweet smell of her blood

was filling the air. But she did not die that night! It would be

him that would lose his life! I swooped down into the alley and

landed a few feet behind the man. My landing was so quite he

didn't know I was there. But she had seen me and I watched as

the tears rolled down her cheeks. I cleared my throat on purpose

just to get his attention. He quickly looked behind him and seen

me, he shouted, "What do you want! Go away or you will be

next!" I began to laugh loudly and said, "Let the woman go and

I will let you have all the fun you want with me! We will have the party of your life!" He released the woman and she fell to the ground. I yelled to her to get out of there and she took off running. Once she was gone and safe I turned to the man and said, "Are you ready for the party of your life?" He came up and grabbed me. He slammed me into the wall. I whimpered just to make it look like he was winning. He breathed into my face, his breath was harsh smelling of booze and cigarettes. He said, " You know, that was very foolish of you! Because once I have had my fun with you, I am going to kill you." I looked at him and smiled, just enough for the points of my fangs to show and said, "Remember, I told you I was going to give you the party of your life? I forgot to tell you it will also be the party of your death!" I grabbed both of his arms and swung him around slamming him into the wall he had just been holding me against and said, "Let's party!" I slammed his head to the side and struck, sinking my fangs deep into his throat. The blood began to flow over my lips and I sucked it down. But I would not

drain him right then. I was going to have some fun. I picked

him up into my arms and leaped into the night sky. Camaz soon

joined me and asked, "What do you have in mind, my dear?" I

laughed and said, "We are going to have some fun first and then

I will let you finish draining him." So I carried the man off into

the nearby forest. We soon reached a clearing deep within the

woods. We floated down to the ground. The man stared up at

me with horror in his eyes. I said, "So, Mister Murder Man, are

you ready to party with me? I will tell you how this game is

going to play out. We are going to give you a ten minute start

and then we are going to start hunting you. Run as fast as you

can, because once we find you, you will cry for death!" About

twenty minutes later we caught up with the man. He had hidden

himself up in a tall tree. I knew he was there because I could

smell him. I told Camaz to circle around the tree and I would

attack from the air. I leaped up into the air and soared high above the tree. The man didn't see me so I landed on the branch

next to him. I startled him so badly he lost his grip and fell

toward the ground. But before he hit Camaz grabbed the man in

mid-air and floated back down to the ground. I landed beside of

them and said to the man, "Sorry, but the party is over!" At that

moment Camaz sunk his fangs into the man and drank him dry.

Once finished he dropped the man's body to the ground, smiled

at me and said, "That was quite fun my dear, we should do this

more often!" I looked up at him, smiled and said, "I agree my

love and you know what else?" "No what?" "This whole

adventure has made me quite horny!" Camaz quickly took me

into his arms and we tumbled to the ground ripping at our

clothing until we were completely naked. Camaz was on top of

me looking down and said, "My god you are as beautiful in the

moonlight as the first night I met you!" I reached up, pulled him

down to me and began to kiss him madly. I felt him enter me

and I screamed his name into his mouth over and over as the

orgasm racked my body. We arrived back at the castle a few hours later and entered our chambers for our long sleep of death. Daylight was approaching so we did not have much time left. We both showered and got into our bed. I quickly fell off to sleep in my loving husband's arms.

Chapter 29

LOUISA AND RICHARDS WEDDING

The day had finally arrived! Louisa and Richards wedding.
Louisa had ask me to be her maid of honor so I had been
upstairs with her getting ready. Her gown was stunning. It was
strapless with pearl inlay through out the top and the bottom
was flowing white satin. The gown clung to her body perfectly.
Atop her head was a crown of Diamonds and Sapphires. Her
long black hair was pulled up in an intricate braided bun and the
veil was tucked under the crown and flowed down her back to
the floor. I had chosen a Sapphire blue gown with matching
heels. Because it was a royal wedding, I wore my crown as
well. Camaz entered our room to see if we where ready. I told
him he looked very handsome in his tux and we only needed a
few more minutes. As I adjusted the bottom of her gown and the
train I lifted up her dress and slipped a garter belt on her leg .

Then I looked up at her and said, "That's mine, I want it back!"
We both laughed and then the music began to play. Once we
reached the bottom of the staircase Camaz went to Richard's
side and I slowly walked down the isle to my spot. Then they
began to play the wedding march and Louisa almost floated
down the isle as she approached with such grace. The wedding
vows were said and the high counsel pronounced them wed and
King and Queen of England. The reception was grand. There
were many old friends from our past there to wish the
newlyweds good luck. We even met some new friends who
we had invited to our homeland. Sarah and James were from
Scotland and the rulers of that country. Camaz and James hit it
off from the beginning But Sarah and myself took a little longer.
Louisa had always been my best friend from the beginning and I
was so sad that I would not be seeing much of her anymore. But
by the time the night was over Sarah and I had became good
friends. The next evening when we awoke we made ready to

leave England and return to our homeland. We said our goodbyes to Louisa and Richard. They were getting ready to go on their honeymoon to Rio. Richard owned a small island off the coast and everything had been made ready for their arrival. I hugged my best friend and told her to have fun. Also that I was going to miss her. She hugged me back and said, "You are the best friend a girl could ever ask for!" She kissed me on my cheek and off they went. I thought back to Samuel and Kim's wedding and made a sigh of relief. Thank goodness things had gone well!

Chapter 30

THE GREAT UPRISING

After Louisa and Richards wedding Camaz and I deceived to go
on a second Honeymoon of our own. I had always wanted to
go to the Amazon, so he had made arrangements with some
friends he knew there for us to visit. We arrived in a small
encampment in the Amazon jungle and where greeted by two
very fierce looking women. Camaz introduced me to them. The
first was very tall and muscular woman with milk chocolate
colored skin. She had long black hair that was braided down her
back. Her name was Aello witch meant whirlwind. She had been
named for one of Hippolyte's Amazons who was a fierce
warrior. The other woman was of slight build and her name was
Echephyle her name meant Chief Defender. They invited us to
go hunting with them later that evening ,but first they wanted us
to meet their council. We arrived at a large cave entrance and

descended down into the darkness. After walking for about thirty minutes we arrived at a large cavern. There was many Amazon vampires about the cavern. In the amazon culture there was no king and queen, they where ruled by their council. The head of the counsel's name was Orellan he had been in charge of the council for over 1000 years. He was tall and well built for a warrior. But it was explained to me like the human Amazons, the vampire women did all of the fighting. We where told there had been a great battle for many years with a neighboring tribe to the east. Just recently they had lost one of their most valuable warriors Antiope. She had been ambushed while out scouting for invaders. Everyone there was saddened at her lose. They where making ready to attack the neighboring tribe that had taken her life. That evening Aello took us out into the rain forest to hunt for our meal. She explained there were many evil humans there for us to hunt. There was a lot of drug cartel in the forest. Suddenly I caught a whiff of something wonderful in the air. It had made my throat burn wildly just thinking about it! I

dropped down into my hunting crouch and began to follow the

delicious smell. Aello and Camaz had also picked up on the

smell and were hunting as well. After a few minutes we came

upon a clearing. There were many men there with guns and

drugs. It looked like they were getting ready to make a

shipment. The smell of evil permeated from them. Those men

had killed many men, women and children. The scent was so

strong, it hung heavy in the air. I signaled Camaz and Aello to

go around to the other side of the encampment. There were a

total of twenty in all. More than enough to go around! I sprung

into the air and floated over head. I honed in on my target and

swooped down grabbing the man and soared back up into the

sky with him in my arms. The man was so startled he was

motionless. While still in flight I sank my fangs into the softness

of his neck and began to feed. Once I had drained him I let go

and let him fall back to earth. I could hear screaming and

gunfire from below. I looked down and the camp was in total

mayhem. I swooped back down and went for my next victim.

He was a large man with the belly of a beer drinker. I was not

interested in his blood, for I was full, so I just landed on him and

snapped his neck. Suddenly I felt something sharp plunged into

my back. I swung around and came face to face with my

attacker. It was not a man, it was a demon. I knew because of

our friends back home. I reached behind me and felt the cool

silver spike he had plunged into my back. Lucky for me he had

missed my heart. I pulled the spike from my back and began to

circle the demon. I had been well trained in battle against

demons so I knew how to handle him. I did not have my sword

with me that night, I did not think I would need it. So I used the

next best thing, the spike. Demons are fast but not as fast as we

are. I darted in at him and plunged the spike deep into his neck.

He screamed out and began to back up. I attacked again and

plunged the spike into his heart, he fell to the ground dead. The wound in my back had begun to ache. I sat down to steady myself. I heard Camaz calling my name. I called out to him, "I am over here." He came running up to me and said, "My dear, are you alright?" I looked up at him and said, "Damn demon staked me in my back!" Camaz came over and assessed the wound in my back. He said, "Darling we need to get you back to the Amazon's encampment and have this wound taken care of!" He picked me up in his arms and took off running. I laid my head against his chest and closed my eyes. The pain in my back had become unbearable. I whispered to Camaz, "Please hurry, I do not know how much longer I can take this pain!" Camaz began to run even faster. Aello was right beside us and was telling me everything was going to be alright. They had healers in their encampment. Camaz later told me the spike the demon had used was silver and it could have been deadly if he had struck my heart. My recovery took a little over two days and I was as good as new. Camaz told me they had finished off the rest of the men when he found me. There would be no more killing and drugs coming from those men again! About a week later we meet with the council and were ask if we would help them with their battle against the neighboring tribe. Because of everything they had done for me we could not say no. That evening we had met with the council to plan our attack. As I said before, the battle would be fought by the women. The men were to stay behind and guard the encampment, protecting the young ones. But Camaz would be coming with us. We traveled about twenty miles and reached the neighboring tribes border. In all there was two hundred of us. As I looked down on the tribes village I could see many amazon warriors ready for our attack. There numbers where about even with ours. Aello had told me the leader of the opposing clan was Sabin and they had been mortal enemies for many hundreds of years. She had found out it was Sabin who had killed Antiope. Aello vowed she would be the one to take her life. So we began our decent down to their encampment. They were aware of our coming and had made ready for battle. We rushed at them full force and engaged them in battle. Camaz and the other men had to stay back and couldn't interfere in our battle. I drew my sword from my back and took on the first enemy amazon I came upon. She was very tall and muscular. She swung her sword at me and missed, for you see I was very fast! I circled around her and took her head off. I then went on to the next one. After about an hour the battle was over. Many had died on both sides. Aello had Sabin down on the ground and was readying for the killing blow. I heard Sabin say to her, "Go ahead and take my life, as I have taken you friend's, but remember, we have all lost greatly!" Aello looked down at her enemy and said, "Sabin I will not take you life today, but if you or any of you people harms mine I will be back!" Aello then stepped away from Sabin and walked over to me. She says, "Come, lets gather our dead and leave this place of death!" So we gathered up all of the dead and wounded and headed back to her home. Later on I talked with Aello and asked why she had spared Sabin's life. She told me she had tired of all the bloodshed and just wanted peace. A few days later we were on our way back home.

Chapter 31

OUR WELCOME HOME

We arrived back home the following evening to a great welcome home party. All of our family and friends were in attendance. Kim came up, hugged me and said, "Welcome home! We have been so worried about you!" I smiled at her and said, "It is good to be home, It has been a very ruff three months!" She pulled me over to the table where Samuel, Mikel and Iris were sitting. I took a seat next to Iris and Camaz joined us. It was so great to have all our family around us. Kim told me her and Samuel had something very important to tell us. She told us while Camaz and I had been gone they had selected a surrogate to carry their child. She had already been impregnated and was due in a few weeks. I smiled, hugged her and said, "Wonderful news my dear! I have been so ready for great grandchildren!" She smiled and said, "I knew you would be happy!" Samuel called order to the party and proposed a

toast to his beautiful wife and future son or daughter. Everyone

raised their glasses and toasted the happy couple. The music

began to play and Camaz reached for my hand and said, "May I

have the honor of this dance?" I placed my hand in his and said,

"Why yes kind sir!" Then, before I knew it, Camaz had me

whirling around the dance floor. It turned out to be a wonderful

evening. Especially with the happy news. Once we said our

goodbyes to everyone, we left to go hunting. After we arrived

back home and were in our chambers for our long sleep. I asked

Camaz a question, "Love, after everything that we have been

through, do you regret taking me as your wife and queen?"

Camaz looked at me strange and asked, "Why would you ask

such a thing! I have loved you since the first day I laid eyes on

you. I knew that you where my soul mate and had to have you!

Please never doubt my love for you!" I rolled over and he took

me into his arms. I kissed him softly and said, " I am just

talking silly, I know that you love me as I love you, but we both have come so close to death and I cannot bear the thought of losing you. If I did I could not go on without you!" Camaz held me tighter and said, " I thought that was what you were so concerned about. But I want you to make me a promise, if I should die before you, please stay alive for our children, grandchildren and great grandchildren to come please my love!" I shivered in his arms at just the thought of me having to go on living without my beloved Camaz. That night Camaz made love to me like the first night I had been made vampire. So gentle and passionately. As I fell off into my sleep of death I smiled at the thought of how much this man loved me! The next evening when we arose, there was a great commotion. Someone was yelling our names. We sprung from our bed and dressed quickly, then raced off to see what was wrong. When we reached the great hall everyone was gathering. We went up to Samuel, Kim, Mikel and Iris to find out what had happened. Kim was frantic!

She told me the surrogate that was caring Samuel's child had been kidnapped and they had been unable to locate her. This had brought back bad memories of her kidnapping and I tried to calm her. Camaz was talking to the council and warriors readying to search for Katina. We all fanned out in different directions to try and locate Katrina. Kim had given us a piece of Katrina's clothing so we could scent her. For you see, each vampire has their own special scent. Camaz and I took off into the woods stopping every few miles to test the air for her scent. I picked up on something and stopped dead in my tracks, taking in a deep breath and caught her scent. It was very faint but enough to follow. I signaled Camaz to follow me and we took off running again. As we traveled the scent became even stronger, but there was another scent we had picked up on. The scent belonged to a vampire. But one we had never encountered before. I stopped and asked Camaz if he knew the scent. He thought for a moment then answered, "No my dear, I am not familiar with this scent." I then said, "We must hurry, we do not know who this vampire is and what he is doing to the poor woman!" So we took off running toward the scents we had picked up. We arrived at a clearing in the woods near the face of a mountain. There we saw an opening to a cave. The scent was very strong near the opening. I drew my sword from my back and made ready for anything. Just then Samuel and everyone else arrived. Camaz told them Katrina was being held inside the cave by a vampire had never come across before. We made ready to storm the cave when someone yelled out, "Do not come any closer or I will kill the woman and child!" Samuel yelled to the vampire, "Who are you and why have you taken Katrina from us?!" We heard the vampire laugh and then say, "Katrina is mine! I have loved her for a 1000 years, but she would not even look at me. But now that I have her, I will never give her up!" Samuel yelled, "You know that you cannot hold any vampire against their will, also she is caring my heir, if any harm comes to her or my child I will kill you!" "Then so be

it, come little king and try to take back what is yours!" Samuel

started to head for the opening to the cave, but I stop him and

said, "Samuel, please do not go in there, let Camaz and me go. I

promise one of us will bring her out safely!" Samuel was not

happy with my request but he let us go. Camaz went in first

with me close behind. We both had our swords drawn. It was

very dark in the cave, but our eyes adjusted quickly. From the

corner of my eye I caught something flash by quickly. I swung

around and took my fighting stance. Camaz did the same and

we where back to back, ready for the attack. Then the vampire

showed himself. He was very old, much older than Camaz. He

looked to be of Brazilian decent. He had long black hair that

was pulled back and tied with a leather strap. His eyes where a

few shades lighter than Camaz's. His body was muscular and

tan. I could tell he was a made vampire not born. He looked

at us and began to speak, "Welcome former king and queen,

could the king not come and fight his own battle?" Camaz

hissed at him and said, "Where is Katrina? If you have harmed

her in any way, you will not leave this cave alive!" The vampire

laughed and said, "Powerful words. Let me introduce myself,

my name is Raulo. I was made vampire in 1160 by the great

warrior King Miguel Otello. I am not afraid of you or your wife.

But I must say she is quite stunning. I will kill you first and then

have some fun with her before I take her life!" Camaz yelled at

Raulo, "You will never touch her!" He then ran toward the

vampire with his sword swinging. The man sidesteped Camaz

and turned to me. I raised my sword to protect myself. He came

at me with a vengeance. He swung his sword at my head but I

was to quick for him and he only caught me in the shoulder. But

it was a deep wound and was bleeding badly. I swung around to

face my attacker again, but before I could Camaz was on him.

They began circling each other, swinging their swords. I knew

Camaz could handle himself. So I went a little deeper into the cave to try and find Katrina. A few hundred feet in I found her huddled in a corner. I went up to her, introduced myself and told her we need to get out of there. She was very heavy with child, so she could not move as fast as I could. We reachrf the area where I had left Camaz in battle with the vampire and the scene was crazy. Camaz had the vampire on the ground with his sword to his throat. But Camaz had many wounds of his own and he looked very weak. I can tell that he had lost a lot of blood. There was a deep gash on his belly and another just below his neck. It was taking everything he had just to hold the vampire down. The vampire had both of his hands on the blade of Camaz's sword, preventing him from taking his head. I told Katrina to stay put and I ran over to where the two men were. I raised my sword and slash downward, taking off the head of the vampire. Camaz in his weaken state fell off the vampire and laid on his back looking up at me. He then said, "Woman you are amazing!" I smiled at him and said, "Anything for the man I love!" I called the others into the cave to help with Camaz. He

had many wounds and it would take awhile for them to heal. By

then the wound in my shoulder had begun to really hurt. The cut

had gone all the way to the bone. I sat down beside my beloved

and said, "Aren't we a pair, always getting ourselves cut up!"

Camaz laughed and said, "Yes indeed, that we are!" We arrived

back at the castle and the healers begun to work on us. Katrina

had been checked out. Her and the baby were fine. She only had

one more week till she would give birth so she had gone to her

quarters to rest. The healers had closed all of our wounds, but

we had to finish the process by exchanging our blood. So we

retired to our rooms to finish the healing process. Camaz laid

me down on our bed and removed my clothing. He kissed down

my neck to the wound in my shoulder. He bit his wrist and

allowed the blood to flow into the wound. He then kissed me

gently again. He laid down beside of me and awaited my

healing blood. Camaz's wounds were much worst than mine so

I turned and offered him my neck. He gently bit down and began to drink. We had only done that several times before and every time it brought a great burning way down low. I grunted with the passion that was building between my legs. Camaz released his grip on my neck and said, "Oh my, what was that my dear? Are you trying to tell me something?" I looked up at him and smiled, "Oh, I don't know, maybe!" I then grabbed him and pulled him down to my mouth kissing him madly. I felt his hands caressing my breasts and that ignited my passion totally. I whimpered and said to him, "Take me! I need you now!!" Camaz entered me and we made love like there was no tomorrow.

Chapter 32

THE ROYAL CHILD COMES

It had been a little over a week and Katrina had summoned

Samuel and Kim to her chambers. The royal child had been

born. It was a precious little girl. She had her mother's dark

brown hair but she has Samuel's and Camaz's emerald green

eyes. Katrina handed the child to Samuel and said, "Here is your

little princess."Samuel took the child from Katrina and looked

down on her and smiled. He then said to Kim, "Come my

darling and hold our child for the first time." Kim walked over

to Samuel and took the little girl from him. She looked into the

face of that little angel and said, "Oh my god, she is beautiful!

Look Samuel she has your grandfather's emerald green eyes!"

We said our farewells to Katrina for she would be leaving to

return to her home. We all went downstairs to introduce the

child to the council. Samuel and Kim had already chosen a

name for the child. So Samuel went up to the council and

announced, "Members of my counsel, may I present to you,

Princess Arora." He held the child up for all to see. There was

great cheering at the announcement of the new princesses name.

The council pronounced her princess of Mexico and possible

future queen of the kingdom. Kim and myself said our farewells

to everyone and went to their chambers with Arora. Kim had

already created the nursery right off of their bedroom. She laid

the baby down in the crib and we went over to the bed to talk.

Kim was beaming with pride and joy. She told me, "Oh Anne

you have no idea how happy I am! Arora is so beautiful!" "Kim

I know just how you feel, the first time I laid eyes on Mikel I

just fell in love. I was not sure if not being his biological mother

would cause me to no want him, but he smiled up at me and

stole my heart! The same thing happened when his sister came

along! I think it had something to do with those emerald green

eyes! That was the first thing that drew me to Camaz." Kim

chuckled lightly and said, "Yes, I know what you mean. The same thing happen to me when I starred into Samuel's eyes!" So we spoke for a little while longer then I told her that Camaz and I were going to hunt. I went back downstairs where Camaz and Samuel where talking. I let Samuel know that Kim was awaiting him in their room with the baby. So he quickly left us and went upstairs. I asked Camaz if he was ready to hunt, that I was so hungry and he said yes. So off we went for our midnight meal. While we were hunting Camaz asked me if I was happy living here in Mexico. He knew how happy I had been when we were living in the mountains of North Carolina. I told him it did not matter where I lived as long as I was with him. I would always be happy. He smiled at me and said, "My one true love, I would take you anywhere you would be happy. If you would like to go back to the states then I shall take you there!" I looked up at him and smiled, "Now, love, you know I cannot leave the children! Other than you, they are my life! But I would like to go somewhere for a few months. Were it would only be us. Like the island we have off the coast. We have been through so much in the last year that I would just like to get away from everything!" Camaz took me in his arms, stroked my cheek and said, "If that is what your heart desires, then that is where we will go!" He then kissed me gently and whispered "I love you with all of my heart, always have and always will!" After a few minutes of intense kissing I broke our embrace and sniffed the air. I then turned to him and said, "Oh goody, dinner! Let's hunt I am famished!!" I leapt into the air with Camaz right behind me. I tested the air for the scent and begun to follow it. We were deep over the jungle when I spotted where the scent was coming from. Below us was an encampment of about six to eight men. The looked to be drug smugglers. The air was heavy with the evil within them. It was driving my senses crazy! The flames of thirst were rising in my throat. All I could think about was quenching them! The fever had taken over me and I swooped down toward the men on the ground. I had chosen the

first one on the left. I landed on him and knocking him to the

ground. He was so startled that he doesn't even fight me. I

struck and drank him dry. Camaz had finished his first and was

working on his second. The other four men were now armed

with guns and had begun firing at us. I took one in the chest, but

bullets do not harm vampires. The other men were firing at

Camaz. He had already grounded another and had started to

drink. I yelled, "No fair, that is three to my one!" So I went

after my second one. He was a fighter, so it made the pleasure

of feeding so much better. The harder they fight, the quicker the

heart races, causing the blood to flow quicker. I had him

drained in a matter of seconds. There was only one man left,

he had tried to hide in the forest, but had no idea we could track

his every move. He had hidden himself in a thick undergrowth

and was trying not to move. Camaz was on one side of him and

I was on the other. We slowly moved toward the man till we

were almost on top of him. He looked up at us and in Spanish said, "El Diablo !" I smiled at him and said, "Close." I then jumped on him, slamming his head to the side and drank him dry. Once we had finished with all of the men we headed back home. The next evening we would begin planning for our much needed vacation. I was so excited I was going to be alone with my loving husband on a deserted island. Just him, me and the beaches. I loved the beach at night when the moonlight was shining on the water!

Chapter 33

MOONLIGHT BEACH

All had been made ready for our trip to the island. We had said
our goodbyes to everyone and would be leaving in a few hours.
A few weeks before we had a crew go out to the island to make
it ready for our arrival. We would be taking the powerboat to
reach the island. We could have flew but I so loved riding in the
boat with the wind blowing in my hair! I also loved the smell of
the salt air. We arrived on the island around 3am. Everything
was still as I remember it. The house sat close to the beach and
the front was all glass. There is something I have not mentioned
up to this part of my diary. A few years back we learned that we
where able to go out in the sunlight. It had something to do with
the time I was plunged into the great darkness. I'm not sure if it
was the transfer of our blood or if it had something to do with
the darkness itself. But it was possible for us to be in the sun.

But we do not do it at home, for we must keep this a secret. If our enemies where to find out, they may try to duplicate the process. Also if humans were to see us in our true form it would frighten them. For you see when we are in the sunlight, our pale skin glows red. Camaz told me the first time he saw me in the sunlight it startled him. But he said he loves my glowing red skin! We found out by accident one morning when we were arriving back from a hunt. It was almost daybreak when we came upon a wounded women in the woods. It looked like she had been attacked by some kind of animal. We could not leave her there to die. So we decided to take a chance and get her to the hospital. After we dropped her off, we headed back into the woods knowing we would not make it back to the castle in time. We were deep in the woods when the sun broke. I was so afraid to die, but Camaz held me in his arms, telling me he loved me and we waited for death. But it did not come. We stood there in the sunlight looking at each other in astonishment. We

both say at the same time, "Why are we not dead and why are
we glowing red!" So now you know how we are able to be in
the sunlight. We went to our room and made ready for our sleep,
we would only sleep for a few hours because I wanted to enjoy
the sun on my face again. We awoke around 2pm and went
outside to enjoy the sun. We laid on the beach holding each
other soaking up the rays. After about 20 minutes we went for a
swim. We played in the ocean for hours. Then it started to get
dark. I was beginning to get very hungry. I told Camaz that I
was ready to hunt. So we jumped into our powerboat and headed
back to the mainland. We had been on the island a little over a
month when we had visitors. Mikel and Iris had come to let us
know there was a problem back home and the council had
requested our return. Oh well, so much for my two month island
vacation. But we could always come back. Being a retired king
and queen didn't mean we still did not have responsibility.
So we packed up the speedboat and headed back to the

mainland. We arrived at the castle a little after 3am. We went

straight to the main hall to meet with the council. We were told

a great blackness had fallen over the land. Many humans were

being slaughtered for no reason and they had been unable to find

out who had been doing the killing. At that point all they could

tell us was that who ever it was, was not human. They had not

been able to find out if it was vampires. The bodies were so

ripped up that no visible bite marks could be located. Just then

we received word there had been another attack in a neighboring

village. Many men, women and children had been massacred.

We got our gear on and left to search for that monster or

monsters. A few minutes later we arrived at the village. There

was bodies everywhere. They were so mutilated it was hard

to believe they were human. We all fanned out around the

village trying to locate who had done this. I was in the woods

trying to scent whatever the creature might have been. I tested

the air for anything and then I caught it. The scent was very faint but it was there. The attacks had not been done buy vampires for the scent I picked up on was werewolf! I went deeper into the forest following the scent. I had never smell such ugliness in a werewolf before. The werewolf had to have been a very evil man when he was human. His scent caused my throat to burn and my hunting instincts to kick in. I dropped down into my crouch and moved forward. I called out in my head to Camaz that I have found the beast and to come as quickly as possible. I was crouched low behind a tall tree when I saw the beast. He was over seven foot tall and massive! I reached behind me and pulled my sword from it's sheath. The beast had a woman from the village cornered and was readying for the attack. I leapt into the air and screamed, "Get away from her!" I landed in front of the beast and swung my sword at his throat, but he stopped my blade between his massive paws and yanked it from my hand. I was so startled by this that I began to back up. I was a very skilled fighter in hand to hand combat but I knew I was no match for this monster. He charged at me and I leapt into the air just in time. He missed me and slammed into the tree where I was standing. But that didn't even phase him. He rolled off the tree and looked up at me then in a growl said, "Come down here little vampire, I am not done with you yet!" I yelled down at him, "I will come play with you, if you let the woman go." He replied, "Very well, you seem to be much more fun anyway!" I yelled to the woman to run and she did. The beast looked back up at me and said, "There, I have let the woman go, now you come on down here and let's have some fun!" I knew Camaz and the others were on the way and should be there soon so I lowered myself back to the ground. He growled at me and said, "Now, my lady, shall we dance?" I smiled at him bearing my fangs and said, "Let's do this!" I charged at the beast and sprung into air landing on his chest. He hit the ground hard. I jumped off of him and ran for my sword. He was right behind me, but I was much faster than he was and reached my sword just in time.

I grab it and swing around as he was about to get me. My sword cut deep across his chest and he screamed in pain. But he managed to rake his long sharp claws across my sword arm and then pain took me. He had managed to cut all the way to the bone. I screamed Camaz's name out in my head and I heard him. "I am coming my love!" The beast was on top of me and I was fighting for my life. The damage the claws have done to my left arm had rendered it useless. I used my one good arm and my legs to keep him at bay but the blood loss was beginning to take it's toll on me. I started to weaken and then I felt his fangs at my neck. My god, he was going to rip my throat out! I screamed as I felt his hot breath at my throat and then everything went dark. Again the darkness, but wam I alive or dead? I couldn't hear anything as before when the darkness took me. I must have been dead. Then I heard something. Someone was in the darkness with me. It was that terrible growl, oh great the beast had joined me in the darkness. The growling was getting louder and closer. But I had no where to hide. It was like I was blind. Then I

heard the voice of my beloved. He was yelling at the beast to get

away from me. Were we all dead and stuck in this blackness of

hell? I could hear the two of them engaged in a great battle. But

I couldn't see what was going on. Then I heard the beast roar and

then scream. Then there was silence. I waited to hear anything

that would tell me my Camaz was okay. But I heard nothing.

Then a few moments later I heard a whisper in my ear, "Hold on

mother! We are takingyou back to the castle." It is Mikel, his

voice was such music to my ears! I waited to hear Camaz's

voice but I heard nothing. I called out to him in my mind,

"Camaz , please answer me, please tell me you are okay and that

I have not lost you!" I begun fighting the darkness trying to get

out of it. Little by little my senses returned to me. I opened my

eyes. I was in our bed and there was many around me. I scanned

the room looking for Camaz but I was unable to locate him. I

knew something is wrong. Camaz would never leave my side. I

looked up at Mikel and asked, "Where is your father?" Mikel looked at me with sad eyes and my heart broke. He said, " When we arrived father and the werewolf were in a great battle. You were gravely wounded. Father was fighting with all his might to keep the beast away from you. He told us to take you and go. That we must get you to safety first. So we brought you back to the castle and then went back to help father. But when we got there he was gone. We have been looking everywhere but have not been able to locate him. We found the beast dead a few miles from where we found you. But there was no trace of father." I closed my eyes and ask everyone to leave me to my grief. I laid in our bed thinking what was I going to do with out Camaz! He was my whole life, my everything! I could not believe he was gone! I called out to him in my mind over and over but there was no answer. I told myself that as soon as I was healed I would go out and look for his body. I would bring my beloved back home to us. I then begun to cry, but not normal tears, but blood tears.

Chapter 34

HUNT FOR CAMAZ

A few days later after I had completed the healing process I left the castle to search for Camaz's body. I had gone back to the original place where the battle had happened. This was very hard on me, but I had to do it. I would not rest until I found him. I begun testing the air for his scent. There was a faint smell of him and the beast so I followed it. I reached the area where the werewolf's body was found. I searched all around the area but was unable to locate Camaz. So I begun to fan out in a circle, all the while testing the air for him. Further and further out I went until I picked up on a faint hint of him that I had not smelled before. I begun to follow it. The farther I went the stronger the scent became. After about two miles I came upon a clearing. His scent was very strong there. In the far corner of the clearing was a large fallen tree. I raced to the tree for I knew this was where I would find my beloved. I reached the tree and found Camaz lying on the other side. I dropped down onto my knees beside of him and began to weep. My heart was breaking. I had loved this man since the first day I laid eyes on him! I reached for his face and stroked his cheek saying, "My beloved, I am so happy I have found you! Now I can take you back home to rest in the place you loved the best!" I got to my feet and picked him up into my arms to carry him home. But when I did that he moaned! Oh my god! He was not dead!!!! But I could tell he did not have very long. So I laid him back down on the ground. He had brought me back from the darkness and I would try to bring him back. Even if had meant giving all of my blood to him! He had many massive wounds all over his body, so I started with the worst ones. I bit into my wrist and begun to pour my blood into the wounds. As I moved on to the next one the others begun to close. Once I had finished with his wounds the next step was to get him to feed from me. It was going to be very hard as weak as he was but I had to try. I knew I was very weak from the

blood loss already but I had to try. I bent down and whispered in

his ear, "My darling, if if you can hear me, I have started the

healing process. But you need to feed." I offered him my neck,

but he did not bite. He was still to weak so I took my sword

blade and cut my neck. Allowing the blood to flow into his

mouth. After about five minutes he begun to suck very weakly,

but at least he was feeding. I was beginning to become very

weak, He must have sensed this because he stopped feeding. I

felt his hand upon my cheek. I opened my eyes and looked

at him. He was looking much better. I whispered to him, "My

love you need to feed more." He smiled at me and said, "You

are my life, I will not take yours! I am feeling much stronger

now so I have no more need for your blood." I looked at him

and said, "Are you sure your alright?" "Yes my dear, but I will

need you to hunt for the both of us. We both need to feed." "But

Camaz, I cannot leave you here alone!" "My dear, I will be

alright, so go." I made Camaz as comfortable as possible and then went off to hunt. About an hour later I found my pray. I drained him quickly so I could continue to hunt for Camaz's meal. I finally find him about an half hour later. I couldn't kill him, for Camaz had to drink from a living person. So I knocked the man out and flew with him back to where I had left Camaz. I laid the man down next to Camaz and said, "Here my darling, drink and get well for me!" Camaz took the man and drained him quickly. Afterward we laid in each others arms. I told him I thought I had lost him forever and my heart still ached because of it! He took me in his arms, kissed me gently and said, "My love, I thought the same thing of you when the beast ripped your arm almost off. I could not let him get to you again. I told you I would protect you with my life!" He kissed me again but that time with great passion. I guess he was feeling better!

Chapter 35

A HAPPY HOMECOMING

We stayed in the forest for two more days and then headed back to the castle. When we arrived everyone was so happy I had found Camaz alive! We were greeted with many hugs and welcome homes! Camaz was still weak, so I took him up to our room. He told me that he was okay, but I was not taking any chances. I thought I had lost him once, I would not lose him for real! I got him into our bed and insisted that he stay there until I told him he could get up. He smiled at me and said, "So, am I to be your sex slave then?!" I answered, "You better believe it! I have great plans for you while you are healing the rest of the way!" Camaz laughed at my reply and said, "Well then my little queen, come here and I will service you!" I replied, "With pleasure sir!" I laid down beside of him and he pulled me to his chest. He begun kissing me, first on the lips and then he rolled me over onto my back. He began kissing down my neck and kept going all the way down! As he reached my womanhood I screamed out his name over and over! He continued to let me know just how happy he was to be alive and back with me! The next evening we arose in each others arms. I kissed him gently on his lips and told him how much I loved him. I then asked him, "Do you feel strong enough to hunt this evening or shall I bring someone back for you?" He smiled at me and said, "I am fine my love. We will hunt together." So we got dressed for the hunt. I had chosen one of my most seductive outfits. Camaz looked at me and said, "My god woman, you are absolutely stunning! No man or vampire could resist you!!" "You know, flattery will get you everywhere with me!" "Oh how well I know!" We both laughed and then headed downstairs. We were greeted by our entire family and friends. Mikel and Iris came up to us and told us how happy they were that we were home and save. We all hugged and we said our farewells as we went off to find our next meal. I told Camaz

that I wanted to go into Mexico City to hunt. I was in the mood

for some city food. He laughed and said, "As you wish my

dear." So we took off for the city. We arrived there about an

hour later. We landed atop one of the taller buildings and tested

the air for our prey. I picked up on a scent quickly. It was

coming from a few blocks over. I pointed in that direction to

Camaz and he smiled. So we took flight again and headed

towards that wonderful smell. We landed on the building where

the smell was coming from. We heard the men inside, they were

plotting a murder/kidnapping. There was a very prominent

business man in town. They planned on kidnapping his wife

and holding her for ransom. But they would not allow her to

live, even if he paid the ransom. She had spurned the affections

of one of the men and he had hated her every since. He was

planing on raping then murdering her slowly. This made me so

angry that I began to see red! I told Camaz I was going to go down and knock on the door then ask if I could use the phone.

He gave me the thumbs up and I leapt to the ground. I went

around to the front of the house and knocked on the door. A few

minutes late a dark Mexican man answered the door. I told him

my car had broken down and ask if I could use his phone to call

for a tow. The whole while he was looking me up and down

with hunger in his eyes. He invited me into the house and

showed me to the phone. I picked it up and pretended to call for

a tow. I then hang up the phone. The man asked me if I would

like something to drink. I told him yes and thanked him. He

went off to the kitchen to get the drink. I made myself at home

and waited for his return. He came back into the room with my

drink, sat down beside of me and said, "My god, you are so

beautiful! Do you have someone who tells you that?" I

answered, "As a matter of fact, yes I do!" He smiled at me and

said, "Well that is to bad, because you will not be leaving this

house!" I began to laugh and he said, "What is so funny?" I

answered, "The joke is on you, for you see, you are the one that

will never leave this house!" I then smiled, baring my fangs. He

jumped to his feet and yelled, "What the hell are you?!" I

answered, " I am the hunter of evil men and I am here to take

your life!" I jumped on him so quick he did not see me coming.

I slammed him to the ground with me on top of him. He

struggled, but it did good. I was one hundred times strong than

he was. I laughed and said, "It will do you no good to struggle!

But I will not kill you quickly., I am going to kill you slowly,

just like the woman you where planing on killing!" He looked

at me puzzled and said, " How did you know about that?" I

laughed and said, "Silly man, vampires know and hear

everything!" I then broke his left arm. He screamed out in pain

and continued to scream as I broke every bone in his body. The

whole time he was begging me to kill him. I told him "Oh no,

not yet, you are going to suffer some more!" I then broke his

back. He stopped struggling and began to moan. I slammed his head to one side, struck and began to feed. I finished him in

seconds. When I was done I heard Camaz behind me laughing

he then said, "Looks like you had fun!" I looked up at him and

smiled, "Oh yes, that was the best fun I have had in years!" He

laughed again and asked, "So, my vampire queen, are you

ready to go home?" I answered, "Yes I am. I am ready to be

back in our room with your arms around me and your lips upon

mine!" So we headed back to the castle.

Chapter 36

DO THESE WARS EVER END!

A few months later while we where out hunting we came upon a vampire we had never met before. He introduced himself as Sabor and said he was from the vampire kingdom of Scotland. We said our hellos and introduced ourselves to him as well. He told us of a great up evil back in his homeland and said he had heard of our great battles and his Queen had sent him to ask us for help. We invited him back to the castle and told him we would take it up with the council. Camaz called a meeting of all of the council members and the elders. Also present were Mikel, Iris, Samuel and Kim. We explained what the stranger from Scotland had told us and what he had requested. After a long discussion we were in agreement to assist the Scottish King. A few days later we were making ready for out trip to Scotland. Our plane was leaving at 9pm and we would be arriving at 5am so we had brought our coffins for transport from the plane to the King's castle. The King had made arraignments with local Werewolves to pick us up and transport us to the castle. Later that evening when we awoke we all were escorted to the main hall to met the Queen of Scotland. Sabor welcomed us and introduced us to his Queen Elise. We said our hellos and got down to business. Sabor informed us that they had been under attack by a neighboring Clan and they were trying to over throw them. He had lost many good vampire warriors. The head of the Clan was very old and powerful. Their feud went back centuries. They had fought many battles and there had never been a winner. That is why he had asked for our help. He had grown tired of battle and just wanted it over with. So we studied his battle plan. That evening we went out into the countryside looking for prey. We were not use to the island but our senses had no problem finding prey. There was an encampment of men below us in a valley. From the smell of them they were very bad men. The burn in my throat flared to a full blown fire. I could taste the men on my tongue. We slowly begun creeping down the mountainside toward the men. They looked to be a warrior clan of some kind. I didn't know they still had those types of clans in Scotland. We reached the base of the mountain and dropped down into our hunting crouch. We approached the encampment. The men were making ready for bed and did not see us. I went around to the back of a tent that was already occupied. I could hear the man softly snoring. I took my sword and sliced the tent open and entered. The man was naked and dreaming because his manhood was at attention. I laid down beside of him and begun to stroke him. He moaned softly and then rolled over opening his eyes. He stared at me for a moment then said, "Am I dreaming? My god you are beautiful!" I straddled him and said, "No, I'm afraid your not dreaming, but when we are done, you will know what a nightmare is!" I smiled at him, showing my fangs. He began to scream but I put my hand over his mouth and stuck. His warm, sweet, salty blood begun to flow down my throat quenching my fire. He struggled but then became weak. Finally giving in to me. I drank until his heart stopped. I got up off of him and went out to see how Camaz was doing. He had two men cornered and was getting ready for the attack. I went up to him and said, "Need some help? My, the one on the right looks so juicy!" Camaz laughed and said, "He is all yours my dear!" I went up to the man, he was shaking badly from his fear. I said to him, "Do you know what we are?" He shuck his head from side to side. "We are death, here to pay you back for all of the terrible things you have done!" I then smiled, showing my fangs. I watched as the horror reached his face. He now knew what we were. He begged for his life. I said, "Did you spare all of the people you have killed when they asked for their lives?" I then pounced on him knocking him to the ground. I sank my fangs into the softness of his neck and drained him dry. I looked over at Camaz, he was finishing off his dinner as well. So we headed back to castle to make ready for our next battle. I was growing tired of the fighting. But we were asked to help, so help we did. I didn't tell Camaz I was tired of all the fighting, or he would have made me stay behind while he put his live on the line. I couldn't let that happen, as I had sworn to protect him with mine! The next evening we arose and got dressed in our battle gear. Camaz hugged me and told me I was the best looking warrior he had ever seen! I laughed and said, "you know flattery will get you everywhere with me!" He smiled and said, "Oh, how well I know!" He then kissed me. I broke our kiss and said, "Oh my, want to make love, not war?!" Camaz laughed and said, "If we could, I would, but we must help Sabor." "Oh shoot, just when I thought I had you right where I wanted you! Okay let's go kill us some bad vampires. The quicker we are done, the quicker we can get to the make love part!" Camaz smiled at me and took my hand. So off we went to make war not love.

Chapter 37

THE BATTLEFIELD

We arrived at a large open field just west of where the castle was located. We looked out over the battlefield. There were many vampire warriors on their side. We also smelled werewolves, demons and fairies. But we had brought all of our best warriors with us from home. So we were prepared for anything they might throw at us. I had chosen to take a mount. He was a beautiful sold white stallion with stunning blue eyes. I had always loved horses, so when the queen offered me the mount I did not hesitate. Camaz had chosen a stunning black stallion. We sat next to each other and ready for the battle. We begun our decent down too where the other clan was located. Sabor called the charge and we took off like the wind. My horse carried me directly into the heart of the warrior clan. I had my sword drawn and took out the first werewolf with one swing.

But unbeknownst to me there was another one coming around behind me. He leapt onto my horse and dug his claws into my back. I screamed out in pain and fell to the ground. The pain was unbearable, but I managed to get to my feet with sword in hand. The beast charged me. I swung my sword and removed his head. His body fell to the ground, trembled and then fell still. He had already begun to change back to human form. I could hear Camaz calling to me in my head, asking me if I was okay. I replied back to him that I was wounded but I was still good to fight. I could feel the blood running down my back, but I did not have time to worry about it. All of a sudden I was embattled with a vampire and demon. I was not sure I would be able to fend them off with the blood loss. So I fought with all of my might and skills. I managed to take the vampire out quickly but I was having problems with the demon. He was very fast and I had slowed down due to the blood loss. All of a sudden he sprung at me, knocking me to the ground. I had lost my sword, so I went for my daggers. I managed to bring one around and drive it home into the demon's heart. He shrieked and dropped to the ground. I laid there for a moment trying to catch my breath. I knew I must get up or they would kill me. I leapt to my feet and grabbed my sword. I could see Camaz in battle with a vampire. He looked like he was having problems with that vampire. I ran over to where they were, leapt at the vampire and slashed his chest deep with my sword. The vampire screamed clutching his chest. He backed away from Camaz. I was to find out later that was the enemy clans king. He fell to the ground. I stood over him, ready to strike but Sabor stopped me. He said, "No, I will not have him killed!" He looked down at the king and said, "Michell, I will spare your live if you agree to end this feud! We have been fighting many years and I have grow tired of it. Do you agree or shall I take your life here and now?" The king looked at Sabor and said, "I like you have also grown tired of all the wars. I agree to your terms!" So that was how the war ended. He called a halt to all of his warriors and told them it was over and to go home. Just then the blood loss had caught up with me. I fell to the ground. Camaz rushed over to my side and asked, " What is wrong my love?" "I have lost much blood. The beast that took me off my mount clawed my back." Camaz sat me up and surveyed my wounds. He said, "I am surprised you were able to stand up, let alone fight. We need to get you back to the castle. I need to heal these wounds!" He picked me up, leapt into the sky and flew me back to the castle. Several days later after Camaz had healed my wounds I was ready to travel. So we said our goodbyes to all our new friends and headed back to Mexico. I told Camaz when we got home I wanted to go to the island and spend a few weeks re-coopering. He agreed. He to needed a vacation and would make the plans for our trip when we got back home. After a few days of being home I had fully recovered from my werewolf attack and was ready for our trip to our island.

Chapter 39

OUR ISLAND RETREAT

A few days later we arrived at the island. Everything had been made ready for our arrival. Camaz carried me into the house kissing me the whole way. God I loved this man!! It was so nice to be able to go out into the sun again! I loved the warmth on me and I loved looking at Camaz's amazing body in the sun! Even though he glowed red he was still so hot!! I told him once we got settled in I wanted to go for a swim. There was no need for bathing suits here as we were the only ones on the island. I ran out to the water and dived in. The water there was so warm! The beaches were a stunning white and the ocean was a crystal blue. I loved to go under and look at all of the beautiful sea life! I could stay down as long as I liked because I did not need air. Camaz and I swam for miles checking out all the beautiful reefs and abundant fish. While we were exploring we came across a sunken Spanish freighter. We went inside to explore. From the

look of it, the ship had been down there for hundreds of years

and no human had stepped foot on it since it sunk. So we

explored for treasure. We came across a large chest in the

captain's quarters. We opened it and to our surprise there was

many gold doubloons inside along with many diamonds,

emeralds, rubies and other precious stones. We closed the chest

and Camaz picked it up. We headed back to our island retreat.

About an hour later we arrived at the beach house and brought

our bounty in. We placed the chest on the large wooden coffee

table and went to get dressed. Later that evening we got ready

to go to the mainland to hunt. After our long swim I was

starving! We jumped into the speedboat and headed back. After

we docked the boat we headed into the heart of the city to hunt

for our prey. After a few minutes I picked up a scent. I leapt up

to the top of a building and perched on the ledge. Camaz

followed right behind me. I tested the air for a minute and said,

"There, to the east, a really delicious smell!!" He laughed and said, "Yes, my dear, that it is. It has my mouth watering and there is more than one, so tonight we feast!!" I smiled at him and leapt into the air heading east. We landed on the building where the smells were coming from. We were in a very seedy part of town. We looked below and saw streetwalkers on the corner. A man was talking to them and had invited both of them back to his place for some fun. He had offered them one hundred dollars a piece for the night. They agreed and followed the man to his house. We would save the women. Even though they were streetwalkers, they were still innocents that did not smell of evil. We watched as they entered the house directly across from us. We flew to the roof of the house and then crawled down entering an upstairs window. We crept down the hall, all the time we could hear them talking downstairs. Then we heard the voice of another man. It was very deep with a Spanish accent. The man that invited the hookers into the house introduced the girls to the other man. One of them said, "We

did not agree to two of you for one hundred!" The man that

brought them into the house answered, "That's fine, we didn't

plan on paying you anyway!" The shorter of the two hookers

drew a switchblade from her pocket and brandished it at the

two men and saying, "We are leaving, do not try and stop us!!"

The male with the deep voice laughed and said, "Oh no, you

are not going anywhere!" At that point a third man appeared

behind the woman with the knife and grabbed her, taking the

knife from her. She screamed out and tried to get away, but he

was to strong. He put the knife to her throat and dragged her to

the couch. He then began ripping her clothes off. The other two

men had the second woman down on the ground and were

tearing at her clothing. This was our cue. I look at Camaz and

grinned, "Let's have some fun!!!" We descended down the

stairs and came into the living room, startling the men. One of

the men yelled out, "Who the hell are you and what are you

doing in our house?!" I laughed and said, "I heard there was a party going on and wanted to join you for some fun!" The third man released his woman and told her to stay put or he would kill her. He then came up to me and said, "So you want to party with us? Who is this man? Your pimp?" I laughed and said, "No, actually he is my husband, but he likes to watch." I walked up to the man and he said, "Your husband likes to watch you having sex with other men?" I laughed at him and said, "Why no silly, he likes to watch me kill people. It gets him off" I then grabbed the man. He was startled by my strength and tried to get away, but he was going no where! I slammed him to the floor and straddled him. I then smiled at him bearing my fangs. That smug look of defiance left his face and was replaced with fear. I could smell it on him and it was driving me crazy! But I fought the urge to feed and let him smolder in his fear. He looked up at me and said pleadingly, "Please do not kill me demon, I promise I will not do harm to anyone ever again!" I smiled even bigger and said, "No, sorry, you have done enough killing for two lifetimes and I am not a demon. I am Vampire!!!" I then slammed his head to the side and struck. My fangs dug deep into his neck and his sweet blood began to flow. I could hear his heart as it beat faster and faster, trying to keep up with the blood loss. But it was of no use. I drained him dry! I stood up and wiped my mouth on my arm. I saw Camaz at the other end of the living room, he had the man that brought the women into the house on the floor and was draining him. I looked around the room but couldn't find the other man. I took a deep breath, scenting him out. He had gone upstairs and was hiding in one of the bedroom closets. I told Camaz I was still thirsty and I was going after the other man. He smiled at me and said, "Have fun!" So I went upstairs to the bedroom where the man was hiding. I swung the closet door open and he was cowering in the corner. I grabbed him by the hair and dragged him out of the closet. I looked down at him and smiled. He saw my fangs and grasped. I told him, "We are going to play a game. Can you guess what I am?" He looked at me with fear in his eyes and said, "A demon from hell?" I laughed and said, "Wrong, you lose! I am your worst nightmare come true. For you see, I am Vampire and the destroyer of all humans that are evil!" I raked my fingernails across his chest causing deep gashes. He screamed out in pain. I raised my bloody fingers to my mouth and licked the blood from them. I then smiled and saying, " Wow, your blood is wonderfully evil! You are good enough to eat!" I then slammed my fist into his face, crushing his jaw bone. The blood was pouring out of the wound. I bent down and began licking the blood from his face and then whispered, "Brace yourself, here I come!" I then sank my fangs into his neck and started to feed. He fought me, but to no avail. I savored every drop of his blood, it is so sweet with evil! Finally I finished him. I got up off of the body and headed back downstairs to join my beloved.

After we made the women forget, we head back to the

speedboat and our island. Oh how I loved the night life!

Chapter 40

FINALLY A BREAK

After spending a few weeks on the island I told Camaz I
wanted to go back to our home in North Carolina. We would
make the trip back to the castle to let everyone know we were
leaving. We explained to them that after all we had been through
and almost losing each other, we had deceived to go back to the
states for awhile. They all wished us happiness and said they
would keep in touch. That evening we boarded our plane headed
back to the states. I am sad we are leaving the children and
grandchildren, but we needed the time alone. We knew Samuel
and Kim would rule the country fine. The next evening we were
back in the comfort of our home in the mountains. Oh how I had
missed my beautiful home and countryside! The night there was
just beautiful! After we unpacked our things Camaz asked if I
was hungry. I told him I was famished. He asked if I preferred

country or city food. I told him I preferred to hunt in the city.

There was so much more evil there! So we readied ourselves to

go out on the town. We lived close to Asheville, so that was

where we would be hunting. We arrived downtown a little later

and begun our hunt. We had gone to the seediest part of town,

knowing the prey would be plentiful. We leapt to the top of a

three story building and tested the air for our dinner. The

smell of human blood was overpowering. But I fanned out

farther looking for the special scent of evil. After a few minutes

I picked up on a scent. There was a man and woman off in the

distance and they both reeked of evil! Normally men are who

we kill but every now and then we came across a very evil

woman. Those two were serial killers of the worst kind. They

kidnapped children, torture, rape and then killed them. I had

heard about that pair and was hoping we would run into them!

Their acts made my blood boil!! I signaled to Camaz that they

were below us on the street. I told him I did not want their deaths to be quick, but slow and painful! I wanted to take them back to our home and have some fun before we kill them. We leapt from the roof swooping down and grabbed our pray, placing our hands over their mouths so they couldn't scream. We flew with them. heading off toward home. We arrived there a few minutes later. We were high up on a mountaintop. Humans very seldom came up this way. So no one would hear their screams. We took them into the house and down into the special basement we had constructed with holding cells. I placed my victim in one and locked the door. She was screaming at the top of her lungs. Camaz had the man locked away in another cell. I was starving, but I would only take a little for now. I still had plans for this woman and by the time I was done she would be begging for death. I entered her cell, she was still screaming. I slapped her face hard and she stopped. I then said to her, "So you like to torture and kill innocent little children do you. Well we are going to play a little game you and me. First let me tell you what I am. I know you have heard the myths about

vampires. Well my dear that is what we are!" I then grinned at

her, bearing my fangs for her to see. She whimpered and backed

away from me. I told her, "I will not kill you right now. But I am

hungry!" I went up, grabbed her and forced her head to one side.

I sunk my fangs into the softness of her neck and began to feed.

I listened to her heartbeat so I would know when to stop. After a

few seconds I stopped drinking. I was still hungry, but what I

had taken would do. Camaz had done the same with his victim

and was coming out of his cell. He came up to me and asked,

"So, my dear, what is the plan?" I smiled at him and said, "I was

think a little game of hide and seek. Let's release them into the

woods and hunt!" He laughed and said, "Sounds good to me!

How much of a head start should we give them?" "I was

thinking maybe thirty minutes to make the hunt more fun!" So

we took our pray from their holding cells,went upstairs and

outside. We told them we were going to give them a thirty

minute head start then we were going to hunt and kill them. I told them their deaths were going to be quite painful. I then yelled "Run as if your life depends on it, because it does!" They both took off running at full speed. So we would wait. Camaz cames up to me and took me in his arms. Then he whispered in my ear, "So, what shall we do for thirty minutes while we are waiting?" He then begun kissing me. I laughed into his mouth and said, "And just what do you have in mind husband?" He pulled me closer to him and said, "This!" He began caressing my breasts. I moaned out in pleasure. I dug my fingers into the small of his back and said breathlessly, "I need you now my darling, now!" He picked me up and carried me into the house to our room. He laid me down on the bed and removed my clothes. I watched him take his clothes off, bearing all for me to see. He was so beautiful! He hovered over me staring into my eyes. He grinned and said, "Are you ready for me?" I screamed out, "Yes! Take me now!!" He lowered himself onto my body and entered me. I screamed his name over and over with each stroke until he brought me to climax. I raked my nails down his back causing him to explode. We laid there for a few minutes and then he asked, "Well, my dear, that was quite lovely. Are you ready for the hunt now?" I smiled at him and said, "Oh yes, after all that, I am famished!" He chuckled and said, "Well then hunt we shall!" We went into the woods to hunt for our pray. They had gotten quite a head start, but we pick up on their scent very easily. We began to track them and caught up about two miles from the house. They had been running so hard they had to stop to catch their breaths. They were resting next to a large tree. We didn't want them to see us coming, so we leapt into the air and took flight, landing on a branch above them. I yelled down at them, "Tag you it!" They looked up, startled and took off running. I leapt from the branch and landed on the man. Camaz did the same and had the woman on the ground. By then my blood lust had taken over. I slammed my fist into the man's face, breaking his nose, jaw and knocking out some of his teeth. He screamed out in pain, then begged for his life. I looked down at him, smiled and said, "Did you spare the lives of the children you kidnapped, tortured and raped? Tell me, did you!" I then slammed his bloody face to one side and rip his throat out. The blood poured out of the open wound. I then begun to lap it up laughing the whole time. Camaz was having a great time with the woman as well. She was whimpering as he slammed his fist into her face breaking every bone. I heard them crunch with each blow. He then rippede her throat open and drank deeply. A few minutes later they were both dead and growing cold. I got up off the man and went to where Camaz was standing. He smiled at me and said, "That was the best meal I have had in ages! Her blood was oh so sweet!" I laughed and said, "Sweeter than mine?" He replied, " My love, no ones blood is sweeter than yours!" He took my hand and said, "Let's go home." I planned on spending a lot of quality time with Camaz so I will end my Diary here for now. But soon I will take up the pen

again and tell you of things to come.

Chapter 41

OUR HOMECOMING

This is my first entry into my diary in almost a year. It had been a busy eight months. We had royal births, new marriages and some deaths. So I will began were I left off, my last diary entry. We arrived back at our home early in the morning. The hunt had been such fun! The taste of the two serial killers blood still had my mouth tingling. Oh how sweet they were! As we made ready for our sleep Camaz asked, "Do you think everything is alright back home?" I answered, "The kids can handle themselves and if there was any problems I am sure they would contact us. Stop worry yourself and come over here!" He came to me and sat down. I touched his face gently and smiled. He smiled back at me and said, "My beautiful queen, you are my heart, my life, my everything!" He pulled me to him and kissed me deeply. A few hours later after our lovemaking I fell asleep in my loving husband's arms. The next evening when we awoke Camaz asked me if I would like to go for a run in the woods. I had always loved to run, feeling the wind at my face, so I said yes. We left our house and began our run. Camaz was faster then me but I loved trying to catch him! He slowed just enough for me to catch up with him and just when I was ready to grab him when he sped up and I missed. I was laughing so hard I missed judge my steps and tumbled to the ground. Camaz stopped, ran back to me and asked, "Are you alright my dear?" I answered still laughing, "Yes, just two left feet." Camaz burst out laughing then reached for me and helped me up. Then we were off running again. Oh how I loved to run! After about thirty minutes of running I stopped, tested the air and said, "Can you smell that? Oh my, someone has been very naughty!" Camaz stopped, laughed and said, "Oh yes! They sure have been!" We began tracking the scent until we reached a clearing. There was a small cabin with smoke billowing from the chimney. I motioned to Camaz to go around the back of the

cabin and to await my signal. I could smell two humans inside,

one was a innocent. I readied myself for the game and knocked

on the door. A few minutes later a man answered and asked if

he can help me. I told him I was hiking but had gotten separated

from my group. I asked if he had a phone I could use to call for

help. He invited me in and told me he was going to go get his

cell. As I waited for his return, I could hear the woman in the

other room. She was whimpering and trying to scream but he

had her mouth bound with duck tape. Just then he walked back

into the room and said, "I'm sorry, but my phone seems to have

lost itself. I will try to find it again. In the mean time can I get

you something to drink?" I smiled at him, but being careful

not to show my fangs. I told him, " That would be nice. I am

thirsty!" Boy oh boy was I thirsty!! So he headed off to the

kitchen to get me a drink. I was out the door and back before he

came get back to where I was. I had told Camaz where the

woman was and he was going to rescue her. Once I knew she

was safe, the games began!! The man returned with a soda. My

keen sense of smell told me he had put something in the drink

to make me sleep. He handed me the drink and I thanked him.

Vampires could drink other liquids other than blood, so I drank

it down. A few minutes later I acted like I was getting sleepy. I

told him I was feeling funny and asked, "What did you put in

that drink? I am so sleepy!" I then fell back on the couch and

pretended to pass out. He came over to check if I was out. All at

once I opened my eyes, smiled, baring my fangs and said,

"Surprise!!" The startled look on his face was priceless! I

leaped up, grabbed him, and slammed him onto the sofa. I

pushed his head to one side and stuck. His warm, salty, blood

began to flow. He struggled trying to free himself from my

grasp but to no avail. I could hear his heart beating frantically

as I drew the last few drops from his body. Then it came to a

shattering thud and stopped. I got up off his lifeless body and waited for Camaz. He had taken the woman to safety. I could

hear him coming back to me.

Chapter 42

OUR SECOND GREAT GRANDCHILD

A few weeks later we received a call that Samuel and Kim's
second child was on the way. So we boarded our plane heading
back to Mexico for the birth. We arrived around 10pm that
evening and were met by Samuel and Kim. She was so excited
she could hardly contain herself. The surrogate was upstairs in
the very room that Mikel had been born in many years ago. The
royal princess Silva was in labor and would not allow anyone
to come into the room until after she had given birth. So the
wait began. A few hours later she sent down word that she had
delivered and asked for Samuel and Kim to come up. About an
hour later they came down carrying two babies! I scream, "Oh
my god! Twins!!!!" I ran up to them and looked into the faces
of two little angels! They were twin boys with Samuel's eyes
and Kim's good looks. I said to Camaz, "Oh, dear, look at our

beautiful great grandsons! They have yours and Samuel's

stunning emerald eyes and Kim's stunning beauty!" Even

though Kim was not their biological mother, they still had her

stunning features. I asked Samuel if I could hold the baby that

he had. He handed the child to me. I held him close and told

him how much his Nana loved him! I asked, "Have you two

deceived on names yet?" Kim replied, "Well, it was going to be

Daniel, if it was a boy. So now we have to decide on a name for

the second child. Do you have any idea's grandmother?" I

thought for a moment and answered, "What do you think of

Dempie? He was our great fairy warrior and friend that lost his

life protecting all of us!" Kim smiled and said, "That is a great

name, what do you think Samuel?" He smiled at her and

replied, "Yes, that is perfect! I loved uncle Dempie, he taught

me how to fight and was a great friend to all of us!" So that is

how the twins where named. Prince Daniel and Prince Dempie.

Our double Ds. Kim and myself excused ourselves and took the babies up to the nursery. The nanny was ready with their bottles, their tiny fangs were not developed enough to feed from a human host yet, so they were given the bottle for about two weeks. Then they would be able to start feeding on a living body. As I stood there watching them feed for the first time, I smile to myself. I was so proud of my new great grand babies! Later that evening while we were out hunting I talked to Camaz. "I do not want to leave. I want us to come back here to live for awhile." Camaz smiled at me, took me in his arms and said, "As you wish my queen. I was wondering how long it would take you to decided to stay!" I laughed and said, "You know me well my king!" He laughed and said, "That I do, every inch of you!" He then kissed me passionately. I whispered into his mouth, "Later my love, I am starving!" He laughed and said, "You are always hungry!" So off we went in search of our next meal. Later that evening we arrived back at the castle and announced that we would be moving back home so we could be near everyone. Especially the new babies! Everyone was so excited when we told them. They had all been missing us, but had not said anything knowing all that we had been through and how we needed some alone time. The following week we made the trip back to the states to close up the house and take care of any unfinished business there. I loved the North Carolina Mountains but I loved my family more! So I have told you of the births, now I will tell you of the marriage.

Chapter 43

MIKAL AND IRIS'S OLDEST KRISTEN TO WED

A few months later Mikel and Iris's oldest Kristen came home for a visit. She had a very handsome English gentleman with her. She called a family meeting and announced that she was engaged to be married. She introduced her suitor as Robert. They have been dating for two years and had decided to marry. Robert was of royal blood from the English clan. We had met his parents years back before he was born. They were very good people, so we were very pleased with her choice. Us girls all went upstairs to start planing the wedding. To my surprise a few days later I received word that my best friend Louisa was coming for a visit. I had not seen her since she married. We talked on the phone all the time, but it was not the same without her here! I could hardly wait till she got there! The next day we were busy planning Kristen's wedding. She had asked her mother if she could have her wedding gown. I smiled to myself.

She would be waring the same gown I had worn at mywedding.

Iris and Kim had also! I loved that gow., Louisa had made it for

me. I could still remember standing in front of the mirror and

being stunned at how beautiful it looked on me! The same with

Iris and Kim. The next day Iris brought the dress from storage,

had it cleaned and ready for the bride to be. When Kristen

finally tried it on, it fit her almost perfectly. There would only

be a few alterations to be done and I had the prefect girl for the

job, my best friend! Finally the day of the wedding had arrived.

We were busy getting dressed. Kristen looked absolutely

stunning! She had also asked to wear the crown and matching

jewelery we had all wore at our weddings. I had sent Camaz to

collect the items from the vault. He came back with them. He

looked so handsome in his tux! I had chosen a pale blue gown

that was sleeveless. I had my matching Sapphire jewelery on.

Camaz came up to me, hugged me and said, "My dear, you are

absolutely stunning! No one in this room compares to your

beauty!" I gave him a quick kiss and whispered back, " I bet

you tell all the girls that!" He laughed and said, "Never! I only

have eyes for you!" He went over to Kristen and said,

"Granddaughter you look ravishing! Here I have brought you

something to match that beautiful dress." He handed her the

wooden box that my crown and jewelery was in. She opened

the box and grasped saying, "I remember these, Kim wore them

at her wedding." Camaz smiled at her and said, "Yes, my dear,

all of my girls have worn these. Your grandmother was the first,

then your mother, then Kim. Now it is your turn to carry on the

family tradition." She took the crown from the box and I placed

it on her head. I still remembered when Louisa placed it on my

head. Just then my best friend walked into the room. She was

wearing a dark blue gown in velvet. She smiled at me then said,

"Well best friend, I think we have out done ourselves, she looks

stunning!" I grinned at her and said, " Yes, I agree. She is a beautiful bride!" We all finished putting on her makeup and made sure her hair was perfect. Then we heard the music begin to play. Kristen got up and went to the door. Her father was outside waiting for her. He took her hand and said. "My dear daughter, you look absolutely stunning!" She smiled at him and said, "Thank you father!" All of us girls began our decent down the staircase. When we reached the bottom, all of our husbands took our hands and walked us down the isle. Then the music changed to the wedding march. Kristen and her father came down the staircase. She was absolutely beaming! They came down the isle and Mikel placed her hand into Robert's and the ceremony began. After the wedding ceremony we all filed into the great hall and awaited the happy couple. A few minutes later they came into the hall. Then the party began. There was many vampires from all over the world there for the wedding. A lot of them were old friends and some would be new. Even our old friend Bodgan from Transylvania was in attendance. We were so happy to see him again. He sat at our table and we

reminisced about our great battle. We all made our toasts to the

happy couple and then they said their farewells. They were

going to spend their honeymoon on our island. It was a

wedding gift from us. After the happy couple had left we said

goodbye to all of our old and some new friends. Louisa and her

husband would be leaving the following evening so we had

invited them to go hunting with us. It had been a long time

since Louisa and I had paired up for the hunt. It would be great

fun! The following evening after we awoke we went to say

goodbye to my best friend and her husband. I was so sad, she

would surely be missed. They told us to come to England for a

visit and we agreed for sometime in the future. After we seen

our friends off. We headed back to the palace. I wanted to go

look in on the babies. It had been two months since their births

and they were growing leaps and bounds! For normal parents it

would have been hard to tell the two boys apart. But Kim had no problem, as I didn't. For you see, each vampire had its on

distinct scent, even twins. A human's sense of smell was to poor

to pick up on this trait. But our vampire senses had no problem.

I held Dempie first, he was such a sweet baby! He had Kim's

sweet disposition. Daniel was more like his father, more

demanding, he was going to make a great warrior some day!

But I thought Dempie would be the one to rule our country

someday! After I coddled with the babies for a bit I let Kim

know that we were going hunting. She didn't want to leave the

babies, so she has had her meal brought in. Don't you just love

takeout!

Chapter 44

AN UNEXPECTED DEATH

Now unfortunately this brings us the sad part. The death of a

close and special friend. We had received word from the

Amazon that Aello had been killed in a battle. She was a good

friend and would surely be missed. That evening Camaz made

plans for us to attend her funeral. The amazonian ritual of death

was way different than ours. First there was a great feast in

honor of the dead. Many evil men and women were brought in

from all over the country for the feast. Then they where

released into the jungle and the hunt began. I was going to

enjoy that, I had always loved the chase! Two days later we

were on our plane heading for the Amazon. We were greeted by

our good friend Tomaz, who was Aello's mate. The grief on his

face was heart breaking. They had been a mated couple for over

500 years! When a vampire takes a mate it is for life. They will

be no other to replace the departed one. I feel so sad for Tomaz, they were so happy together. He filled us in on how she died. They had been out on a hunting run when they came upon a group of rouge vampires. They were taken by surprise. Aello fought bravely but one of the vampires managed to stake her in the heart. Then took her head with his sword. I still could not believe she was gone! We were shown to our quarters to freshen up before the great feast. There was many of our old friends there for the wake. Aello was very loved. I am so sad at her passing! She was a great Amazon warrior! We were seated at the table with Tomaz. He looked so devastated! I said to him, "I know you are hurting right now and nothing I say will bring her back to us, but I just want you to know, we will always be there for you!" He gave me a small smile and said, "Thank you lady Anne, that is very kind of you and Camaz." Just then the head of there council began to speak. He praised Aello in all of her accomplishments. Then one by one all of her family and closest friends spoke their words of love for Aello. After the feast we filed out to the great courtyard. A funeral pyre had been erected and Aello's body was in the middle of it. Tomaz picked up a torch and went to the pyre, said a few words about his beloved, then lit the fire. We all stood there and watched as the fire engulfed her body. Afterward we retired back to our quarters. Once in side behind closed doors I said to Camaz, "I do not know if I would be able to do that to you! It was tearing my heart from my chest just watching him in all of his grief! I do not know how I would be able to go on without you! I love you so much!" Camaz took me into his arms and tried to sooth me. He kissed me gently then said, "My heart, do not worry, nothing is going to happen to me!" "But how do you know that, I have almost lost you many times!" "As I have almost lost you. But we are always there for each other so do not worry yourself so much. Come let us go to bed and ready for our deep sleep." So we got into bed and I fell asleep in my loving husbands arms.

Vampires do not normally dream, but that night I had a very strange dream. I dreamed that I was in the blackness again, but I was searching for Camaz. I screamed his name over and over but he did not answer me. At that point I abruptly awoke screaming his name. He grabbed me and asked, "What is wrong dear heart?" I looked up at him with blood tears running down my cheeks and replied, "I dreamed I was in the blackness again. I was searching for you but could not find you. I screamed your name over and over but you did not reply! I was so scared I had lost you!" He wiped the tears from my cheeks and said, "I am so sorry you had such a horrible dream! We normally do not dream but when we go through a great tragedy it happens. But it doesn't mean something is going to happen to me. So stop worrying yourself!" He then pulled me to his lips and kissed me deeply. I let myself open up to him and he told me over and over in my mind just how much he loved me. The next evening we boarded our plane headed back home. I was sad to leave all of our friends, but I was ready to go home.

Chapter 45

HAPPY TO BE HOME

We arrived back home the following evening. Everyone was there to greet us and welcomed us home. We had only been gone a few weeks but the twins had grown so much! They look to be about ten in human years. I hugged them both and told them how much I had missed them! The both hugged and kissed me. Then they told me they had missed me as well. After we said our hellos to everyone we went up to our quarters to unpack. While I was putting things up Camaz quickly picked me up and took me over to the bed. Sitting me down and said, "Wife, I am so proud of you! From the first day you became vampire you have impressed me in all that you have archived! I have a surprise for you." I looked at him lovingly and said, "Oh, you know how much I love surprises!" He laughed got up and went to the dresser. He returned with a velvet box. He handed it to me and said, "Happy anniversary darling!" I smiled at him and took the box. I opened

it, inside was the most beautiful necklace I had ever seen! He

knew how much I loved emeralds. It had diamonds in between

each emerald and at the neck line was a five carat round emerald.

I said, "Oh Camaz, it is so beautiful! I love it! Can you put it on

me please." He took the necklace from the box and placed it on

my neck. He then kissed my neck and said, "I love you!" I turned

to him, pulling him to me and kissed him madly. Three hours later

we were lying in bed and I said, "Now, it is my turn to give you

your present." I rolled over and retrieved a box from the

nightstand. Inside was a special ring I had made for him. The

stone was a black onyx with his crest inlay-ed over the stone. I

had the inscription "My heart, my life, my love." inscribed in the

band. He looked at the ring, reading the inscription and said, "As

you are to me also my dear!" He placed the ring on his pinky,

pulled me to him and kissed me. That evening we went on the

hunt. We had traveled to South America. We had heard there had been a very bad group of men killing down in Santiago Chile. The drug cartel was extremely bad in South America. So it always made for good hunting! We arrived in Santiago around 2am. We disembarked our plane and headed to our villa we had there. Once we had unpacked everything, we got ready for the hunt. A few minutes later we were in the heart of the city. We had set ourselves onto one of the highest building and began to test the air for our prey. I closed my eyes and let my senses take over. The smell of human blood was thick in the air. But I filtered out all the innocents and searched for that special smell of evil. A few minutes later I caught a whiff of something delicious. I looked at Camaz and smiled. He smiled back at me and said, "Yes dear, I picked it up also. My, tonight will be a great feast!" I laughed and said, "I can hardly wait! Let's go!!" So we took to the air in search of our prey. We were in the woods just outside of the town. The smell had became very strong there. I could hardly contain myself! It had my throat on fire! Those were very evil men. I could tell they had been killing innocents for many years over their drug trafficking. I pointed down to a clearing in the woods for us to land. Once on the ground we dropped down into our hunting crouch and began to stalk our prey. Soon we came upon their encampment. There were at least twelve in all that we had picked up on. I turned to Camaz, smiled and said, "Oh goodie, a buffet!" He laughed at what I had said then said, "Variety is the spice of life!" I smiled at him and said, "Let's eat!" We then began stalking toward the men. I leaped up into the air so I could take the first one by surprise. I swooped down, grabbing the man and took him back up into the air. At first he was startled. But then he began to scream. But before he could alert the others, I struck and draining him. I dropped his body in the woods. I headed back to the encampment and Camaz had already taken four. I've got to catch up! Five down and seven to go. I landed on the ground and grabbed another. He had a large machete and was trying to sing it at me. I took it from him and slashed him across the neck. His neck was bleeding profusely. The blood lust then took over me. I grabbed him and drank him down. Once I had drained him, I dropped his body and headed to where Camaz had his fifth on the ground and was draining him. I ran up to him and said, "No fair, I have only had two!" He looked up at me and said, "I am quite full my love, you may have all of the rest." I looked at him and said, "You are such a gentleman! I love that about you!" So off I ran to get the other five. When I had finish I felt so full that I could hardly move. Camaz found me where I had dropped the last man. He looked down at me and said, "My god woman, you are absolutely glowing!" I look up at him, smiled and said, " My dear heart, I am so full I do not know if I can get up from this place!" He laughed and said, "Very well then, I will carry you." He picked me up into his arms, leaped into the air and flew back to our villa. The next evening we made ready to hunt again. As I had said before, the prey was very plentiful there!

Chapter 46

A NEW KIND OF BEAST

After about two months in South America we headed back home. I had missed the children very badly. I wanted to see the twins and how much they had grown. We arrived back at the castle around 1am. There was much going on inside. We rushed in to find out what it was. We were greeted by Mikel. He told us there was a new beast terrorizing the mountainside. They had not been able to track it as there was no scent. There had been reports that this creature had huge wings and would carry off unsuspecting villagers. The creature only attacked at night, so no one had been able to identify what it was. We told Mikel to gather all of our warriors and meet us in the woods. We went up to our room and put on our battle gear. We had to hunt down this beast and kill it before it could harm anymore humans. We met up with all of our warriors and began our search for this new creature. We all fanned out, taking a section each of the countryside. If that beast stuck, we would be ready for it. They all had been given instructions to sound the alarm if they spotted the beast. We arrived at the area we had chosen to protect. There were many innocents in that village and we were sworn to protect them. Camaz and I had placed ourselves on top of two buildings and were scouring the skies for that monster. Our eye sight is very keen so we would spot it before it could reach the village. About twenty minutes later I spotted something in the sky coming toward the village. I yelled to Camaz that the creature was coming. He contacted the others to let them know we had found the creature and they were on the way. I readied myself for the attack as the creature got closer. I got a good look at the thing. I had never seen anything like it! The beast was green. He had a huge head full of razor sharp teeth, a short stocky body and huge wings. I yelled at Camaz, "What the hell is that?" He replied, "I do not know. I have never seen anything like that in all of my almost 900 years!" I leapt up into the air, drew my sword from my back and made ready to attack. Camaz had done the same and we waited to do battle with that monster. The beast spotted us and roared. It had chosen to attack me first. I guess because I was a woman he thought I was weak. Boy was he in for a surprise! He swooped down with his claws extended. He was going to try and grab me. But I was to fast for him. I shot straight up into the air and he missed me. He roared in anger then spoke, "Come back here! How is it that a human can fly? I have never seen this before!" I laughed and replied, "That is because I am not human. I am Vampire! Do you know what that is beast?" "I have heard of blood sucking demons that live off humans. Is that what you are little one?" "Yes and what may I ask are you?" He laughed and said, "I am the great Canto, demon of legends. I have awakened and I am very hungry!" He then dived for me. I tried to avoid him but I misjudged his speed and he grabbed me with those huge claws. He had embedded them in my back. I screamed out

in pain. I could hear Camaz coming, he was yelling in my head,

"Hold on beloved, I am almost there!" The beast looked down

at me and laughed saying, "I am going to rip you to pieces! Are

you ready to die little vampire?" Now I was pissed. I was so tired

of everyone I had fought calling me little vampire! I reached up

and grabbed the beast's leg and snapped it like a twig. He

screamed out in pain and released me. I began to fall to the

ground. The wound in my back was deep and I was losing a lot of

blood. I did not have the strength to stop my fall. But just before I

hit the ground I was caught by my beloved. He landed and asked,

"Baby, are you alright?" I looked up at him and said, "No, the

beast has ripped my back open. The pain is unbearable!" "I must

get you away from here so the beast cannot get at you again. The

others are almost here" He leaped up into the air and took me to a

safe hiding place. He told me to stay put, that he would back

soon. He kissed me tenderly and said, "I love you, my one true love! I will return as quickly as I can, I promise!" Then he was

gone. I laid there on my side trying not to think about the pain in

my back. I wished I could get up and help with the fight but I was

to weak from blood loss. Before Camaz left me, he poured his

blood into my wound to start the healing process. So I was very

worried about him, as he would be weaker from the blood loss.

I could feel the wounds closing in my back. I tried to get up but

was unable to due to the blood loss. Damn I felt so helpless! I

could hear a great battle going on off in the distance. I just

hoped my family was okay, the beast was very crafty. As he

was able to grab me. I could hear the beast roaring and

screaming. Then after a few minutes I couldn't hear anything

but silence. I let my ears range out trying and pick up any

sounds of my family and friends. Then I heard my beloved's

voice in my head. "We are coming my love. We have defeated

the beast!" I replied back to him, "Please hurry, I am very weak

and I do not want the darkness to take me again!" I laid down on the soft grass and stared up at the beautiful night sky. There were thousands of stars shining up there. I smiled to myself, oh how I loved the night. Then I started to slip into the darkness. I started to fight it! I would not let it take me again! Camaz would be there soon and stop it from taking me. A few hours later I awoke in our room. Camaz was sitting beside of me and he was caressing my face. I opened my eyes and smiled at him. He smiled back and said, "Thank god! I thought the darkness had taken you from me again! I could not bear to be without you again!" I tried to sit up but I was still very weak. He lifted me gently so I could sit up. I put my arms around him and said, "Oh Camaz I thought I would be lost in the darkness again, but I fought it to get back to you!" "I knew you were fighting it, you where talking in your sleep. You where cursing the darkness telling it you would not allow it to take you again!" I smiled at him and said, "I am just glad I was strong enough to fight it this time! All I could think about was getting back to your loving arms!" He pulled me to his lips and kissed me tenderly.

Chapter 47

THE TWINS COME OF AGE

It had been almost two years since the twins were born. They had grown into fine young men. Camaz and their father had been teaching them the art of combat. David had become quite skilled in all, but Dempie was still having problems with hand to hand combat. His brother beat him all the time. One day I invited him to go hunting with Camaz and me. We would work with the boy, so he would become better skilled at hand to hand. After the hunt we took him to the clearing where Camaz had trained me. We told him we were going to help him in his training. I said to him, "Okay, so what I want you to do, is watch Camaz and me. We will teach you how to defend yourself." I positioned myself on one side of the clearing and Camaz was on the other. I had told Camaz not to be gentle with me that the boy must see real combat. Camaz laughed and said, "I could never hurt you dear heart, but I will put up a good front for the

boy." Camaz then charged me. I side stepped him, turned and

went on the defensive. He came at me again, I raised my arms in

front of me to fend off his attack. He swung at me and I blocked it

with my arm. I dropped down, rolled and came up behind him.

I swung my leg out, kicking his legs out from under him. He

went down laughing, "Very good my queen!" He was back on

his feet in seconds, coming at me again. He swung at me again

and caught me in my shoulder. I went down hard, but I was back

up and at him again. Dempie was watching very intently.

Camaz came from behind and grabbed me, holding me tight. I

broke his hold and dropped down from his grip. I rolled to one

side and I was back on my feet again. I said to Dempie, "See

son, it is fairly easy, if you know how to handle yourself. Now

would you like to try with Camaz?" He looked at me and

smiled. He went over to Camaz and said, "I want to train with

great grandmother and you. Can you teach me now?" Camaz

smiled and said, "Yes, your training will begin now." He then

leaped at Dempie. But Dempie had remembered how I avoided

Camaz's attack and sidestepped Camaz, swung around and

landed a blow in Camaz's chest. I clapped and saying, "Very

good Dempie, now your getting the hang of it!" He smiled at

me then went on the offensive again. They trained long into the

night. By the time we were done, Dempie was quite skilled in

hand to hand combat. We all headed back to the castle for our

long sleep. The next evening we arose to the sound of yelling.

We quickly got up and dressed. We headed upstairs to see what

all the commotion was about. Dempie had his brother on the

floor and was fighting him. Dempie was winning! Daniel was

yelling at him to get off. I went over to the boys and told them,

"That is enough horse play you two!" They both laughed and

said, "Yes ma'am, your wish is our command!" Everyone

laughed at what the boys said. We all adjourned to the living

room to plan the boy's party of manhood. I was so proud of

those boys! It was now a week later and the party was that

evening. All had been arraigned for the boy's coming out. I had

chosen a dark emerald green gown for the occasion. I was

wearing the necklace Camaz had given me for our anniversary.

I had my crown of emeralds and diamonds atop my head. I was

standing looking at myself in the mirror. Just then Camaz came

into the room. He was in a black tux and had a small box in his

hand. He came up to me and said, "My dear, you are stunning in

that gown! I have brought you something." He handed me the

box and I opened it. Inside was a pair of pear shaped emerald

earrings and a matching bracelet. I smiled at my loving husband

and said, "Oh my, dear, they are perfect!" I placed the earrings

in my ears and Camaz latched the bracelet to my right wrist. He

kissed the back of my hand and said, "Anything for my

stunning queen! My dear, you are as beautiful as the day I met

you!" We then headed down to the ballroom. There was already

quite a few vampires there from other lands. Some had brought their daughters, hoping to catch one of the boy's eye. We went to our table and took a seat next to all of our family. The boys looked so handsome in their tuxes! Samuel and Kim called the party to order and made a toast to their sons on their coming of age. We all raised our glasses to the boys and cheered. Then the music began to play. Camaz stood up and reached for me and said, "May I have the honor of this dance beautiful lady?" I smiled up at him and placed my hand in his and said, "Why yes fine sir, I would be honored!" Camaz took me out to the dance floor and began swirling me around. I loved dancing with my man! He was so graceful! After dancing a few times we went back to our table. Later in the evening we noticed Dempie talking to a very pretty girl. They seemrf to be getting along beautifully. I scanned the party for Daniel but he was no where to be found. I looked at Camaz and asked, "Have you seen Daniel? I cannot locate him." Camaz smiled at me and said, "I saw him earlier with a very beautiful young lady. I'm not sure where they have gone off to." A few hours later we spotted Daniel on the terrace speaking to his young lady. I pulled at Camaz and said, "I am starving, let's hunt!" He laughed and said, "Always thinking about your stomach! Okay, let's go." So off we went into the beautiful night.

Chapter 48

A CHALLENGE FOR THE THRONE

While we were out hunting one night we came upon a group of vampires that was also hunting. They stopped to say hello and we talked for a bit. It seemed we had a problem. They were there to try and take over the throne. We didn't let them know who we were so we could get more information on their plan. We asked if they were aware the castle was very well protected. We pretended to hate the king and queen to gain their trust. They asked if we would like to join them in the take over. From what we were told they had someone inside that was feeding them Intel on what goes on in the castle. So we had to be very careful. We needed to find out who in our coven had turned traitor. We agreed to meet them back in the same spot the next night to discuss the takeover. We were told their inside man would be with them. We said our goodbyes and headed back to the castle. We had to alert just our family and closest friends. We had no idea who their inside

person was, so we couldn't take a chance of him finding out. We

called a meeting with everyone we trusted and explained what we

had found out. Our good friend John, head of our council, was

away at the time. So we could not inform him. We told everyone

of our plan to find out who the traitor was. We were going to pose

as fighters for their cause and find out the information. We

explained we were to met with them the following night to go

over their battle plan. We would have all of our warriors planted

in the woods ready for the attack. Once we found out who the

traitor was we would signal for the attack. After the discussion we

headed to our room for our long sleep. While I was getting ready

for bed I asked Camaz, "Do you have any ideas who he or she

is?" "No, not in the least. But we will find out tomorrow and take

who ever it is out! No one threatens our kingdom!" I laughed and

said, "I love it when you talk war! It get's me so hot!!" Before I

could blink I was in his arms and he was kissing me madly. Our hands were everywhere. Once we had undressed ourselves he laid me down on the bed and looked down at me and said, "You are my heart. I will love you for all of eternity!" I smiled up at him and said, "As I will love you my one true love!" Then he showed me just how much he did love me. Oh what a night! The next evening when we arose and we got ready to go met the clan planing on taking over our kingdom. I had placed my sword in it's sheath and let my long hair flow over it down my back. I had chosen a long sleeved sweater to conceal my daggers. I looked at Camaz and asked, "Are you ready?" "Yes, my queen, I am ready to get this over with! How dare them threaten us and the traitor is going to pay with his life!" We met up with the others downstairs and made ready for our battle. Camaz had given strict orders no one but him would take the traitor out. We all went outside and took to the air. Everyone had their placement and were to wait for our signal. A few minutes later we arrived at the destination. We landed just out of sight, so not to be seen. We searched their encampment for the traitor and then we spotted him. It is Elder

John! I couldn't believe he had betrayed us like that! I began to

see red, how dare he threaten my family! I begun to go forward

but Camaz stopped me and said, "No, dear heart, he is to strong

for you. I will take care of him. But you have your choice of any

of the others!" I replied, "Good, I'm ready to kick some butt!" He

laughed and then pointed for me to go around to the other side

of the encampment. Once I reached my goal he gingerly walked

out from his cover and approached the men. Elder John looked

stunned. The man we had spoke to the night before came up to

Camaz and welcomed him. John yelled at the man, "Get back!

That is the former King and if he is here his Queen is not far

behind!" Camaz smiled at John and said, "Now John, is that any

way to greet your former king?" John began to back up. But

before he could even start to run, Camaz was on him and had

knocked him to the ground. That was my cue. I leapt from my

hiding spot and went for the man that had invited us there. He looked startled, but then he side stepped me. I stopped behind him and turned to attack again. I was welding my sword as I came at him. I swung for his head, but he moved quickly and I missed. He had drawn his sword and readied himself for battle. I charged him again and caught him across the chest. He screamed out in pain, but he swung, catching me in my arm. The sword had cut deep and I was bleeding badly. But I could not stop or he would have surely killed me. I ran at him again, but this time when he sidestepped me I adjusted and swung. My sword sliced though his neck like it was butter. His head fell to the ground, followed by his body. I looked over to where Camaz was. He was deep in battle with John. They both had taken some very nasty blows but Camaz was winning. I took the shirt off of the body of the vampire I had just killed and wrapped it around the wound on my arm. I then ran to help Camaz. He was on top of John and was getting ready to deliver the fatal blow. Camaz screamed at him, "Why John? Why? We have been very good to you and your family! Now you leave me no choice but to take your life!" John stared into Camaz's eyes and said, "Because you have everything I have ever wanted! Including your beautiful wife! I have desired her from the first day you brought her to the council for our approval. So go ahead and kill me. I have nothing to live for anyway!" I could see the anger in Camaz building. I had never seen him so angry! He yelled down at John, "How could you lust after my wife! How dare you. She is my soul mate and one true love! I am sorry old friend but you have brought this upon yourself!" Camaz then raised his sword, swung, taking John's head. Later that evening when we were alone in our room I asked him why he had been so angry with John. I had no interest in any man, let alone him. He told me when John told him he had desired me that the jealousy took him over and he had seen red for the first time in his UN-dead life. He said that even the thought of another man lusting after me drove him crazy. That night he made mad passionate love to me. As if it was our first time. I kept telling him over and over

he was the only man for me and that there could be no other.

Chapter 49

A WELL DESERVED VACATION

After the battle with John we decided to take a vacation for a few weeks so we could heal from our wounds. I told Camaz I had always wanted to see Paris and he said, "Then you shall! I will make the plans and we will leave in a few days." I was so exited, I had always heard tales of the great city of Paris and I knew the hunting would be wonderful there. A few days later we where on our plane heading for Paris. I told Camaz I could not wait to hit the stores in Paris. That I was ready for some new outfits. He laughed and said, "What ever my queen's heart desires, I will provide it!" The flight took a little over 18 hours, so we retired to our sleeping quarters in the belly of the plane. As I laid in my loving husband's arms I thought about all the wonderful things we would be seeing and with that I fell off into my sleep of death. We awoke the next evening with the feel of our plane touching down at the Paris airport. We got up, dressed and went up to

depart the plane. Once we had gone through customs, we were

met by our driver who took us to a chateau that Camaz had

bought just for our trip. The home was so lovely. Everything

had been made ready for our arrival and we settled into our

new home for the next few weeks. I was starving so I told

Camaz I wanted to hunt before we went shopping. He laughed

and said, "Always thinking with your stomach first my dear!" I

laughed and said, "But darling, I am so hungry and I have heard

the food in Paris is glorious!" He laughed again and took my hand

saying, "Then come my vampire queen and taste all that Paris has

to offer!" So we left our chateau and headed into the city.

Everything was so beautiful there! We could see the Eiffel tower.

I pointed to the top and we both leapt in the air, landing on the

very top. We then let our senses scan out for our prey. After a few

minutes I picked up the smell of something delicious. I said to

Camaz, "Oh my, that smells heavenly! My mouth is watering just thinking about it!" He smiled at me and said, "Yes, I agree, it is quite mouth watering. Shall we go find out what that wonderful smell is my dear?" I reached for his hand and said, "Yes, let's take flight, I can hardly wait!" So off we flew following that wonderful smell. We have reached the outskirts of town and the smell had gotten very strong. We came up on a two story villa and landed on top. We could hear people inside. There was four evils and two innocents. I told Camaz I was going to go knock on the front door. I then leapt from the roof and landed on the ground below. I checked myself to make sure I look good, then headed for the front door. I knocked and waited for someone to answer. A few minutes later a tall very muscular man answered. I told him I had lost my way and asked if I could use his phone. He invited me in, all the while he is eying me up and down. I could feel the lust behind that stare. Once inside I scanned out looking for the others. I found the two innocents in a upstairs bedroom. The were both female and they were bound and gagged. I called out to

Camaz in my mind letting him know where to find the women.

While he was rescuing them I would keep the evils busy. The man

lead me into the kitchen where the phone was located. The other

three men were seated at the kitchen table. One was short and

stocky, another was tall and thin, but the third man was huge! He

was at least seven feet tall and weighed about 300 pounds. He

reminded me of the werewolf that I had fought with and had

almost lost my life over. The man that brought me into the kitchen

told the other men that I had lost my way and needed to use the

phone. He winked at the other men. But he didn't know my

vampire eyes were very observant. I prepared myself for the

game. How I loved the game! All at once all four men were on

me. They tried to knock me out, but I broke free from them. They

stared at me in disbelief. Then the large one said, "How in the hell

did you break free from us?" I laughed and said, "Why my dear

fellow, I am vampire. I am 100 times stronger than you four put

together!" The short stocky man then said, "There is no such thing as vampires!" I turned to face him and gave him my best smile, baring my fangs. He shut up and began to back away. The other men said, "What is wrong with you man?" He replied, " Fangs! She has Fangs!!" I turned toward the others and smiled for them as well. Boy talk about a funny scene. I thought they were going to run each other over trying to get away from me! I went for the big boy first. By the time I was done, Camaz was going to have to carry me home again! I left the other three for Camaz. I couldn't be greedy! I thought big boy would have plenty of blood to fill me up. I leapt at him and knocked him to the ground. He started screaming. I laughed and said, "Oh shut up, you sound like a little girl!" I then smashed my fist into his face to shut him up. After a little more fun I stuck and began to drain him. All the while he is whimpering, begging for his life. But it did no good. I had him drain in a matter of seconds. While I was dining on big boy Camaz had returned and was making a quick ending to the other three. After we finished we left the house and headed back to our chateau. I told Camaz on the way, "Oh how I love

Paris after dark!" He chuckled and said, "Okay my Parisian

vampire queen, lets get you home, I have plans for us and the

night is not over!" The next evening I told Camaz I wanted to go

shopping. He asked, "Are you not hungry my dear?" "No not

right now, I am still full from big boy last night!" Camaz laughed

and said, "Okay, then we shall go shopping my queen." We

arrived downtown it was just after 8pm. All of the stores were still

open. The first store we entered was a dress shop. I picked out a

few outfits and went to the dressing room to try them on. I came

out to model each one for him. The first was a midnight blue

evening gown. I knew he would like this one because he loved

dark blue on me. I twilled around for him to see. He said, "My

dear, you are ravishing in anything you wear. But I have to admit,

that color of blue is stunning on you!" I smiled at him and said,

"Why thank you kind sir!" After about an hour I had chosen three

outfits and we were ready to leave. Our next stop would be the jewelery store. I had to have matching jewelery for my outfits. When we entered the store we were greeted by a very refined Frenchman. He introduced himself as Claude and asked what we were looking for. I explained to him that I was looking for Sapphires and diamonds. Also Emeralds and diamonds. He took us over to a display case that was full of beautiful Sapphire jewelery. I picked out a beautiful Sapphire necklace and matching earrings. I also spotted a emerald cut sapphire ring that I fell in love with. We told Claude we would take those items and then asked to see the emeralds. He took us to another case. I stared down at all of the beautiful items. I spotted an emerald encrusted tiara that I had to have. I also picked out a necklace, earrings and bracelets to match. Being a former queen of Mexico had it's perks! We left the store and headed back to our Chateau to put everything in the safe. Then we headed out for the hunt. The next evening when we arose we head off to the airport to go back home. I'm going to miss Paris!

Chapter 50

BOY DO I HATE THE COLD!

A few months after we returned from our trip to Paris I decided to go out hunting on my own. Camaz had been called away on business a few towns over and I was alone. The children did not want me to go out on my own but I told them I would be okay. That turned out to be a big mistake! I made the trip into town and began my hunt. I had picked up on a wonderfully evil smell just on the outskirts of town. I let my nose lead me to my next meal. I landed on top of a small house and tested the air to see if my prey was inside. I picked up on him right away and he was alone in the house. I slipped into an open window on the second floor and began to stalk my prey. Just as I was getting close to him I picked up on another smell, it was that of a vampire! I began to back away, to go back to the window I had entered, but was grabbed from behind. This vampire was very strong! I fought with all of my might but was unable to break free from his grip. Just then the human I had been tracking entered the room. He was a large Mexican man with many tattoos all over his body. He said to the vampire, "Well, I see you have caught our little vampire queen! We need to get her out of here before she can summon her husband!" The vampire then spoke in a American accent, "Yes, we need to be on our way. It will not take long once she has sent out her distress call to him." At that point the vampire did something to me. I'm not sure what, but I was in the darkness again!! God would it never end! I cried out to Camaz in my head over and over that I had been taken. But did not know where they where taking me. That the vampire had done something to me and I had been swallowed by the darkness. Even though I was plunged into the darkness. I could tell we where on an airplane, but that was all I could gather. I yelled out to Camaz to let him know that I was on a plane, but had no idea where it was going. A few hours later I began to come out of the darkness. I opened my eyes and stared into my captor's. He was a rugged looking

vampire. He looked like a cowboy of some kind. I spoke to him

saying, "Who are you and where are you taking me?" He laughed

and said, "My name is Richard. I have been vampire for a little

over 900 years. I was born to two royals in the United States. I

am taking you back to my home. You are mine now and your

husband will never find you!" I screamed at him, "How dare

you take me from my home! My husband will rip your head

from it's shoulders!" He then laughed again saying, "Little

one, he will never find you! I am taking you somewhere very

special. Once there, you will become my woman!" I looked at

him like he was crazy and said, "Are you nuts! I am married to

the former King of Mexico and our children and grandchildren

rule the country! My husband will hunt you down and tear you

from limb to limb!" He laughed again and said, "Possibly but

he has to find you first!" At that point I just shut up and began

to think. I knew we were on a plane heading to the United

States. I knew the vampire was from somewhere there was western people. I began to listen to the plane's engine and counted time. After about eight-teen hours we touchdown. I was put back into the darkness again! But as I was taken off of the plane I could tell it was very cold there and by listening to the plane and the direction it took I could tell I was somewhere in Montana! The only airport that I knew of in Montana was in Billings. I was taken to an awaiting car and off we went. All the while I was giving this information to Camaz in my head. I just hoped he could hear me! I could now feel us going down from the airport. But after a few minutes we made a turn and started to go up again. I knew the Billings airport sit atop a cliff wall called the Rim. When I was still human I had visited family there once. I knew there were many caves through out the cliff walls. I had a feeling that was where we were going. A few minutes later the car stopped and I was lifted from the car. The darkness still had me so I was unable to see where we were going. It was so cold there! Even for me! I had always hated

cold weather!! We began to descend down into what I presumed

was a cave. We traveled for about forty-five minutes and then

stopped. I was placed on something soft. A few minutes later I

began to come out of the darkness. How was he doing that to me!

From what I knew of the darkness, it only took you when you had

been gravely injured! How was this possible! I opened my eyes

and let them adjust to the darkness. We were in a large cavern that

was dimly lit. I looked around surveying my surroundings. There

were many furnishings in there that looked of Indian background.

I had been placed on a large bed in the corner of the cavern. The

vampire Richard was sitting next to me. He began to place his

hand on my face, but I pulled away saying, "Do not touch me!

I swear if you try anything I will rip your face off!" He smiled

at me and said, "You are mine now little one and I will do as I

please with you!" I began to scream in my head to Camaz that

the crazy vampire was going to rape me! Then I heard him! "I am coming my love! Hold on, fight as hard as you can to keep him off of you!" I screamed to him, "Please hurry, he is very strong and I do not know how long I can hold him off!" Just then the vampire slammed me down onto the bed. I began to fight fiercely. He began to rip my clothes off. I was kicking him, trying to get away, but he was to strong! He was on top of me then. I screamed out Camaz's name as Richard took me. I was fighting him all the while, trying to get him off of me. He was not being gentle and I was beginning to get scared. He had his hands around my neck. Oh god, he was going to try and bite me! Now I was really fighting him. I managed to get him off of me by kneeing him in the gut. I jumped up and ran as fast as I could toward the entrance of the cavern. But he was on me in a flash, grabbing my hair and dragging me back to the bed. He slammed me down and said, "If you try that again, I will kill you!" He then began to try and rape me again. I closed my eyes and cried out for Camaz. Then I felt Richard's weight come off of me. I opened my eyes just in time to see him fly into a wall. Camaz was on him like a mad man! He

was slamming the vampire's head into the stone wall over and

over. I laid there stunned at what I was seeing. Camaz had the

vampire by his neck and was dragging him toward me. I looked

into my beloved's eyes and they were glowing bright red! He

had his sword in his other hand. He handed it to me and said,

"For what he has done to you, it is your right to take his life!" I

looked up at Camaz, he could see the pain in my eyes. This

angered him even more. He slammed Richard down in from of

me. I raised the sword and with one quick swoop I removed his

head. Camaz sat down beside of me and wrapped a blanket

around my naked body. He then took me into his arms and began

to rock me and said, "I am so sorry my love that I did not make

it to you in time! I would have given up my life to keep that from

happening to you!" I looked up at him with blood tears running

down my cheeks and said, "It is alright my love, you saved me.

That is all that matters!" He picked me up and carried me out of that terrible place. Once outside he leapt into the air and flew me back to our plane. Once we had boarded and headed back home I told him that I want to take a long hot bath. I needed to get the nastiness off of my body. Camaz drew me a hot bath, then placed me into the tub. He began to wash me. I had always loved when Camaz bathed me, because I knew what would happen afterward. But I was not in the mood for that after all I had been through and he didn't even ask it of me. How I loved that man! After my bath we both laid down in our bed and awaited for our sleep of death. Tomorrow evening we would be back home.

Chapter 51

A NEW FACE

We arrived back home at midnight. Everyone was there waiting on us. Kim ran up to me, hugged me and told me how happy she was that I was safe. The pain of the ordeal was still fresh on my face and she saw it. She said, "I know you have gone through a great deal, so I will not ask about it. But I am so happy you are home and safe!" I smiled at her then responded, "Thank you for understanding. It was a terrible ordeal and I am just happy to be home with my family and friends!" I excused myself and went to our quarters. Camaz told me he would be down soon. Once in our room I broke down. I began to cry. I knew I was safe, but the fear was still there. I had been violated in the worst way. I could still feel him forcing his way inside me. I did not want to deny Camaz, but I did not know if I could handle sex right then. I knew he would understand, but it was still unfair to him. I went into the bathroom and started a hot bath. I could still feel his nastiness on me and wanted to scrub myself clean. A few minutes later there was a knock on the bathroom door, "My dear, are you alright? Can I come in?" I answered, "Yes, my love, please come in." He came in and sat down on the edge of the tub. He smiled at me and said, "You are so beautiful my queen! I am so sorry you had to go through that ordeal. I promise I will never leave you alone again!" I looked up at him with tears still in my eyes and said, "It is not your fault baby. I should have not gone hunting by myself!" He wiped the tears from my cheeks and said, "I hate seeing you suffer this way! I will never let anything hurt you every again!" He began to wash my back. I loved when he bathed me, but I knew what that lead to and I was scared. But he didn't attempt to arouse me. He helped me out of the bath and dried my body off. I put on my robe and went into our bedroom. He asked me if I was hungry I told him yes, so we got ready for the hunt. A few hours later we were deep in the city looking for our next meal. We sat atop a two story building testing the air. A few minutes later

Camaz alerted me he had picked up on a scent. It was coming

from a few blocks away so we took to the air. We landed on top of

the building where the wonderful smell was coming from. There

were two men and one woman inside. All three had the smell of

evil. There was also two innocents inside. A woman and child.

My blood began to boil, they had been molesting the girl child! I

could hear her whimpering in one of the bedrooms. The woman

was in another. I told Camaz I was going for the child and for him

to get the woman. I also told him to leave the evil woman for me.

As she was the one that had been torturing the child! I slipped

into the window of the room where the child was located, grabbed

her and leaped from the window to the ground. Camaz was

waiting for me with the woman. I told him to take them to safety,

but he refused to leave me there alone. So we took the woman and

child to the nearest hospital and returned to the house. The three

of them were still inside. I told Camaz to enter through one of the upstairs windows and I would go knock on the door. Once I knew he was inside of the house I knocked. The woman answered the door and said, "How may I help you?" I told her my car had a flat and I needed to call a tow truck. She invited me in and showed me to the phone. I picked it up and pretended to call for help. Just then the two men entered the room. Both of them were eying me up and down. I gave a small smile, being careful not to show my fangs. I wanted to have some fun with them before we killed them. I asked if I could have something to drink while I was waiting. The woman said, "Sure." Then she went to the fridge. She came back with a beer and asked if that was okay, as that was all they had. I told her that was fine. I took a sip from the bottle, then Camaz walked into the room. They all said at the same time, "Who the hell are you and how did you get into our house?" Camaz laughed and said, "We are your worst nightmare! We are here to pay you back for all of the evil you have done!" I jumped up from my seat and leaped on the woman knocking her to the floor. She screamed telling me to get off of her. Camaz had taken

out the first man by breaking his neck and was now on the second

man. I looked down at my prey and smiled, showing my fangs.

She looked stunned and spoke, "I have had nothing to do with

what these men have done. I have been their prisoner!" I smiled at

her again and said, " I know better. I can smell the pure evil on

you and I know what you have done to that poor innocent child!"

I then slammed her head to one side and stuck. I began to drink

her down slowly. She was struggling to free herself from my grip

but it was to no avail. I drew in her final drop and released her.

Camaz smiled at me and said, "My dear, you are absolutely

glowing! She must have been extra delicious!" I laughed and said,

"Yes she was! So how was your meal?" He smiled at me and said,

"The best I have had in years!" So we left the place and headed

back home. Along the way we met a vampire that was new to us.

She was short and thin. She told us she is new to our country and

asked how the hunting was. We told her the evil was very

abundant in this area. She told us her name was Marylou and she

was from central Florida. We invited her back to the castle and

she agreed to come. Along the way she told us about herself. She

was made vampire in 1926 by a man she though she would spend

eternity with but he left her once he changed her. She then asked

questions about us. We told her we were the former king and

queen of Mexico and our grandchildren were currently ruling the

country. I then told her the story of how Camaz and I meet. Fell in

love and how he had taken me as his vampire queen and mate for

all of eternity. She told us she was happy that we had found each

other and we were so happy. I really liked the woman! We would

soon become very good friends. We arrived back at the castle

and introduced her to everyone. We then excused ourselves to

go change. I asked Kim if she could show our new friend to the

guest quarters. It was still early in the night so after we had

changed we went back up to visit with the family. Marylou was

already talking to Kim when we arrived so I joined in the

conversation. Marylou had told Kim she really liked it there and had ask permission to stay. Kim told her there was a ceremony she had to go through to become a member of the court. But first they would have to discuss it with the council. The council would do a background check on her and her maker. A few hours later we said goodnight to our new friend and headed off to our quarters. Once in our room Camaz took me in his arms and kissed me gently. I began to pull away and he picked up on my distress. But I pulled him back to my lips and kissed him deeply. I could feel the desire building way down low. He lifted me up and carried me to our bed without breaking our kiss. I whispered into his mouth, "I need you badly!" He replied, "Are you sure my dear? I do not want to proceed if you are not ready!" I looked into those beautiful emerald green eyes and said, "Yes, my love, I am sure. I need you and want you now!" That night he made love to me ever so gentle. Making sure that he pleased me in every way. After our lovemaking I fell off into my deep sleep in my loving husband's arms. A few days later we received word from the council that Marylou's request had been approved to become a member of our court. So we had to make ready for her ceremony to become one of us. After the ceremony there would be a great ball in her honor. We had invited all of our friends from around the world. My best friend Louisa was coming! I was so excited!! We had also invited all the eligible males hoping that she would find someone to love her as much as Camaz and I loved each other. There would be royals as well as regular vampire males present. I wanted her to have her pick. The day of the ceremony all of us girls were upstairs getting ready. I had chosen the evening gown I got while in Paris and the matching jewelery. Marylou was dressed in a stunning red velvet gown with matching ruby jewelery. Atop her head was a tiara of rubies and diamonds. My best friend had chosen a pale pink evening gown with matching jewelery in pink diamonds. Once we had finished dressing all of our partners came to retrieve us for the ceremony. Camaz was going to escort Marylou down to the main ballroom then meet back up with me. The ceremony took about thirty minutes. It was proclaimed that Marylou was a member of our court with all of the privileges that went with it. Afterward the ball began in her honor. We were all seated at the main table when the music started. Camaz asked me if I would like to dance I told him I wanted to wait to see if someone asked Marylou to dance. The rest of our family was already on the dance floor. A few minutes later a very handsome man approached Marylou and asked if she would like to dance. Then off they went. Camaz reached for my hand and said, "Shall we my dear?" I placed my hand in his and we went to the dance floor. He held me close and we glided around the room. I loved dancing with Camaz! After a few dances we returned to our table. I looked for Marylou and spotted her in a corner of the room talking to the young man who had ask her to dance. She looked so happy! A few minutes later they approached our table. Marylou said,

"Camaz and Anne I would like you to meet Joseph, he is from Ireland and is a member of the royal family." We greeted Joseph and welcomed him to our home. Marylou would tell me later that there was an instant spark between them and Joseph had ask her to return to Ireland with him. I was so happy for her and I gave her my best wishes on their relationship. I also told her she would always be welcome here if she ever needed to come back. The following evening we said our goodbyes to our new friends as they left for Ireland.

Chapter 52

A WELL DESERVED VACATION

A few weeks later Camaz told me he had a great surprise

for me. He had planned a special getaway for us for our

anniversary. I was so excited, but he would not tell me where

we were going. I knew it would be somewhere warm because he

knew how much I hated the cold. The day of our trip we were

packed and had just boarded our plane. The suspense was killing

me! I gave him my best pout and said, "Please, please tell me

where you are taking me!" He laughed and said, "You do not have

to give me that face, we are going to Jamaica." I smiled and said,

"Oh goodie, I love Jamaican food!" Camaz busted out laughing

and said, "Always thinking with your stomach my queen! I have

purchased a small island off the coast so we can be alone and in

the daylight!" "That is wonderful! I have so longed to be in the

sunlight again!"We arrived in Jamaica the following evening. We took a speedboat to our new island. Once there I took it all in. My

god it was so beautiful there! There was a large house that sat

upon the beach. As we walked up on the porch Camaz quickly

picked me up and said, "Happy Anniversary my darling!" He

carried me into the house. It was so beautiful! There were many

Jamaican artifacts through out the house. He continued to carry

me until we reached the bedroom. There was a large poster bed in

the middle of the room. He sat me down on the bed and went out

to get our luggage. The room had large glass doors that open out

onto the beach. I couldn't wait for sunrise! Just then Camaz

walked back into the room with our things. He placed them on the

floor and came over sitting down beside me. He smiled at me and

asked, "Are you pleased my queen?" I answered, "Oh yes! I love

this place! I cannot wait till sunrise so we can walk in the sun!!"

He smiled at me and said, "But it is still a few hours till sun up,

what shall we do until then?" I grabbed him and pulled him to me

and began to kiss him madly. After a few minutes he broke our kiss and said, "My, my, what has gotten into my beloved?" I laughed and said, "Hopefully you, my king!" Camaz chuckled and pulled me back to his lips and oh boy did he ever get into me! After we finished our lovemaking we laid in each others arms and awaited sunrise. As daybreak came we got up and walked out on the beach to watch the sunrise. I could feel the warmth on my body already. As I had explained previously when we are in the sunlight we glow a pale red. Camaz told me he was still stunned at how beautiful I was in the sunlight. We laid in the sand for a few minutes soaking up the rays. Then we went for a swim. I loved swimming in the ocean. The water was so warm! While we were swimming Camaz told me he had a very special Anniversary present for me. I became very excited and asked, "What? Please tell me, I cannot stand the suspense!" He chuckled and said, "You must be patient my queen, you will find out soon." After swimming for a few hours we headed back to our house. Camaz asked me if I was hungry. I told him I was famished. He took my hand and led me outback to a small building. He smiled at me and

said, "I though you would like to dine in tonight so I have had

some local food brought in." I smiled at him and said, "You think

of everything!" He laughed and opened up the door to the

building. Inside there was two men and oh boy did they smell

heavenly! My mouth began to water just thinking about them! I

went up to the man on the right and said, "Oh my, you have been

a very naughty boy, haven't you?" He looked at me with fear in

his eyes. He began to beg me not to kill him. I smiled at him

baring my fangs. He cowered in the corner. I said, "What about

all of the innocents you have killed in your lifetime. What did you

do when they begged you for their lives? You took them

anyway!" I walked up to him and he began to scream, I told him,

" There is no need to scream, no one can hear you!" I then struck.

His sweet, evil blood, began to flow down my throat, quenching

my thirst. As I finished taking his last few drops I looked over to

Camaz, he was enjoying his meal as well. I winked at him, he released his prey and smiled at me. After we finished our meals

we went into the house to clean up. I took a quick shower to rinse

off. Camaz joined me in the shower and you can imagine what

happened next! When we got out of the shower we went into the

bedroom. Camaz asked me to have a seat on the bed. He had a

surprise for me. A few minutes later he came back into the room

caring a small black velvet box. I think to myself, "Oh goodie a

new ring! I cannot wait to see it!!" He sat down beside of me and

handed me the small box and said, "Happy Anniversary my one

true love!" I opened the box and inside was the most beautiful

diamond ring I had ever seen! It is a three karat diamond that had

round emeralds surrounding it. He took the ring from the box,

removed my first engagement ring and then placed the new ring

on my ring finger. I took my original ring and placed it on my

right hand. That way I could wear both. I smiled at him and said,

"Oh darling, it is so beautiful. Thank you so much!" He smiled

back at me and said, "You are so welcome my queen! I am so

pleased you like it!" I said, "Like it, I love it!!" I told him to hold

on. I went over to my suitcase and retrieved his gift. I handed him

the box. Inside was a emerald and diamond encrusted dagger I

had made special order. On the hilt of the dagger I had our crest

engraved. He smiled at me and said, "Oh my, it is so beautiful!

How did you know I wanted a new dagger?" I laughed and said,

"A little bird told me. When we returned from our last battle

Mikel told me you had lost the dagger I had given you so many

years ago. So I had another made for you. I am so glad you like

it!" He took me into his arms and kissed me deeply. I thought to

myself, "Oh goodie, fun time again! A few hours later I fell off to

sleep in my love's arms.

Chapter 53

DEVASTATION

We spent three months in Jamaica just enjoying each others

company alone on our island paradise. But it had come time

to go home. I would miss that wonderful place. But we would

come back in the future. We arrived back in Mexico around 1am

and headed for the castle. Everyone was there to greet us. I was so

happy to be home! But that happiness would only last a week.

We received word from England that my best friend and her

husband had been kidnapped. So we all boarded our plane and

headed for England. Kim and Samuel stayed behind to guard

our kingdom. We arrived in London around 3am and headed to

their castle. We were greeted by their top adviser William. He

filled us in on what had happened. Louisa and Richard had been

out hunting when they where taken by ghouls and were holding

them hostage. We all loaded up in vans and headed to the

graveyard where the ghouls lived. I still remembered my

encounter with the ghouls in Mexico and how I had almost lost

my head. I was so not looking forward to fighting with them

again! Camaz had assured me he would be at my side at all times

but I was still worried! We all filed out of the vans and headed

into the graveyard. I had already drawn my sword from it's sheath

and I was ready for the attack. As promised, Camaz was right by

my side with his sword drawn. We entered a mausoleum and

descended into the darkness. Our eyes adjusted very quickly and

we began to search for our friends. We came out into the ghouls

lands deep beneath the graveyard. We were rushed as soon as

we emerged. I was taken by surprise and knocked to the ground.

The ghoul was on top of me and had pushed my arms to the side.

He was trying to bite me. I was fighting him fiercely knowing

that if he did bite me, it would plunge me into madness. He was

so close I could smell his foul breath. I was screaming the whole

time. Then he made a minor mistake and I managed to kick him off of me. I took off in a run to retrieve my sword. He was right

behind me. I slide to the ground and he missed me. I grabbed my

sword and came up swinging. I caught him in the neck and

removed his head. It fell to the ground and I kicked it away. I

thought to myself, "God I hate ghouls!!" I looked around for

Camaz and he was in the heat of battle with two ghouls. It looked

like they may have been winning. So I ran to my beloved's side

and took the head of one of the ghouls. Camaz took down the

other ghoul. He smiled at me and said, "My queen to the rescue!"

I laughed and said, "Anything for the man I love and adore!" Just

then I was struck from behind. I screamed Camaz's name and

went down. The ghoul had struck me in the back with his blade

ripping it wide open. Camaz screamed my name and then

attacked the ghoul, taking his head in one slice. He ran to me and

said, "Ann,e please talk to me, tell me the darkness has not taken

you from me again!" I could barely hear him. It sounded like I

was in a tunnel and the darkness was trying to take me. I fought with all of my might to not let it take me again. But it was of no

use! I was engulfed by the darkness. I cried out to Camaz over

and over but I couldn't hear anything. I began to cry. I could feel

the warm blood tears flowing down my cheeks. The only thing I

could think of was not being able to see my loving husband again.

I was going to miss him so! Then I calmed myself. If I were dead

I would not had been able to feel the tears flowing down my

cheeks. That meant I was still in my body. So I opened up my

mind and called out to Camaz. I listened closely and then I heard

a faint call in my mind. It was my beloved! He was calling my

name over and over. He was telling me I was still alive, but I had

sustained a mortal wound. It was so bad it was going to take a

long time for me to recover. I cried out to him to come save me

from this darkness. In a soothing voice he told me he had started

the healing process, but the wound was so severe it is going to

take time for my body to heal. I began to cry, again the blood

tears began to flow down my cheeks. Camaz called to me, "I am so sorry you are suffering in the darkness alone my love. But I am right by your side and will not leave you for nothing!" Then I felt a light pressure on my cheek. He was wiping away my tears! I cried out with joy saying, " I feel you my love! I am going to fight with all that is within me to come back to you from this darkness!" In the darkness I had no idea of the time that was passing. So Camaz kept me informed. He had also told me Louisa and Richard were safe. We were still in England and we would be there until I had come out of the darkness. I then heard my best friend's voice inside of my head! "My dearest friend. I am here and will remain by your side until you come back to us!" I cried out to her, "Oh Louisa, you have no idea how wonderful it is to hear your voice and know you are okay!" So the wait for my return begun. Camaz and Louisa never left my side. All of their meals were brought in. Camaz needed more than she, as he was still giving me his blood for the healing. I had been in the darkness for a little over six months. But I did not fear it anymore because they were both by my side and talking to me all the time. Somewhere into the middle of the seventh month I begun to feel my body calling to me. I was slowly floating downward. Then I was in my body! All of my senses came alive! I opened my eyes and stared into those beautiful emerald green eyes! I tried to rise from the bed, but was still to weak. He reached for me and took me into his loving arms. He rocked me back and forth telling me how happy he was to have me back. I smiled up at him and said, "Oh Camaz, how I have missed you! I thought I would never make it back to you!" He pulled me to his lips and kissed me tenderly. I did not reach full recovery until a year after my attack. We said goodbye to our friends and headed back home.

Chapter 54

OUR WELCOME HOME

We arrived back home the following evening. Everyone was waiting for us. Iris and Kim came running up to me, hugged me and told me how happy they were I was home and save. After we said our hellos to everyone Camaz said, "We are going to our quarters now. Anne is still weak and needs to rest." I looked at him strange and he winked at me. I thought to myself, "Oh boy, I know what that means!" He took my hand and off we went to our quarters. A few hours later I rolled off of Camaz and stared into his beautiful eyes and said, "My goodness, I love you to!" He laughed and said, "I have almost lost you so many times, I could not help myself!" We laid there for a few more minutes then he asked, "Are you hungry my queen?" I smiled at him and said, "As a matter of fact, I am starving!" We got up, dressed and headed off into the night in search of our next meal. We arrived in town twenty minutes later and landed on the closest building. We perched on the edge and let our sense of smell take over. I quickly picked up on a scent. I looked at Camaz and dropped to the street below. He followed right behind me. We began to stalk our prey. There was three of them a few blocks over. We reached the house and listened to who was inside. We were lucky tonight, there was no innocents inside. But the three were pure evil! Camaz entered through an upstairs window and I went around to the front of the house, and knocked on the door. A man came opening the door and asked, "Hello there, can I help you?" I gave him a small smile so not to show my fangs and said, "Yes please, I have lost my way. Do you by chance have a phone I can use?" "Sure come on in." So I followed him into the house. He showed me to the phone and told me he would be right back. I knew he was off to alert the other men of my presence. A few minutes later he came back accompanied by a tall, thin man. He looked like he was on drugs. The first man asked, "So pretty lady, were you able to get a hold of someone to come pick you up?" I made a face and said, "No, I guess they are out right now. Do you mind if I stay here for a bit I have left a message for them to come pick me up." "Sure we don't have a problem with that, do we Juan?" The tall man replied, "No problem at all. Would you like something to drink?" I replied, "That would be nice, thank you." Camaz had alerted me he had already found the third man and had taken care of him. I told him in my mind, "Good, let the games begin!" Just then the tall man came back with a can of soda and asked, "I hope this is okay, it was all we had to drink." I smiled at him baring my fangs and said, "Oh you have something else to drink here I would rather have!" I pounced on him, knocking him to the ground. I pushed his head to the side and struck. I had begun to drink when the other man started screaming. I turned my head slightly, so not to release my prey and saw Camaz had the other man down and was draining him. I went back to feeding from my prey and drained him dry. I released him, stood up and wiped my mouth on the back of my arm. Camaz smiled at me and asked, "Well my dear, did you enjoy your dinner?" I smiled back and responded, "Oh yes I did! He was scrumptious!" He laughed and said, "Shall we go home my queen?" I jumpped into his arms and answered, "Oh yes, I am ready to have some fun!" We left the house with Camaz caring me. he leaped into the air, caring me all the way home. I awoke the following evening in my loving husband's arms. He gave me a quick kiss and asked, "So, what is my lady's pleasure tonight? A night on the town or dine in?"I smiled at him and said, " I am feeling lazy tonight, so let's dine in." He smiled at me and said, "And just what do you have in mind my dear?" I pulled him to me and said, "Oh, I don't know, maybe a little fun later!" He busted out laughing and said, "Your wish is my command!" About an hour later we went down to the holding cells to pick out our main course. After dinner we went back upstairs and talked to the children for a bit. We learned from Kim they had decided to have another child. She just loved being a mother! Their prior surrogate was not available, so she asked if

we knew of anyone. I told her about Mikel's birth mother and we

would send work to her to see if she was interested in birthing

again. A few days later we received word she had agreed and

would be there in a week. So we began making preparations for

her arrival. Little did I know that would be the worst mistake I

had ever made in my entire un-dead life! A few weeks later

Princess Katrina arrived. We had not seen her since Mikel's birth

but she still was as beautiful as back then! We greeted her and

welcomed her back to our home. She was escorted up the the

third floor quarters. The following evening when I awoke Camaz

was not in our bed. I got dressed and went upstairs to find him. I

finally found him in the library with Katrina. My jealousy flared.

I had not had this feeling since her and Camaz went off together

to conceive Mikel! Why was I feeling that! I walked over to them

and sat down. Camaz looked up at me smiled and said, "Good

evening my beautiful queen! Are you hungry?" I said, "Yes my love, I am starving!" He said, "Do you mind if Katrina comes on the hunt with us?" I tried to keep the anger out of my face and said, "Sure, as you wish." He must have picked up something in my voice because he excused himself from Katrina and told her we would be back soon to go hunting. He took my hand and said, "Come my queen, I have something to talk to you about." We left the room and went back down to our quarters. Once we were behind closed doors he asked, "What is wrong dear heart?" I said, "There is nothing wrong, why would you ask?" He pulled me to him and stared into my eyes and said, "I heard it in your tone of voice. I know something is bothering you!" I smiled at him and said, "I know this may sound strange, but when I saw you with Katrina, I became very jealous of you two!" "Why would you be jealous? There is nothing between the two of us! You know I only have eyes from you!!" "I don't know, I guess I am just being silly." He pulled me to his lips and kissed me passionately and said, "My beautiful queen you have nothing to worry about!" So we went back upstairs and readied ourselves for the hunt. I was still not happy about Katrina coming with us, but I would just have to deal with it. While we were hunting I noticed she was staring at him a lot. I knew that stare and I begun to get angry! She had suggested we hunt in the woods because she loved the chase. I had agreed but was not happy about it. All of a sudden I picked up on a smell that was not human. I knew the smell and now I was frightened! For it was the smell of ghouls! I looked at Camaz and yelled, "Ghouls!" But before I could get it out of my mouth all the way, they were on us! Two had taken me down to the ground. One was holding me and the other was trying to bite me!! I was screaming at the top of my lungs for Camaz, but he was also in battle with two ghoul. I spotted Katrina, she was down on the ground with a ghoul on top of her. But their battle looked staged. All of sudden there was a sharp pain in my arm. Oh my god the thing had bitten me!! I remembered Camaz had told me that the bite of a ghoul brought madness. I started screaming for him, "Camaz, help me please, the damn thing has bitten me!" I

had never seen him move so fast! He destroyed both ghouls on

him and was on the ones that had gotten me, ripping their heads

off! Katrina had killed the only ghoul that had attacked her and

she was staring down at me. I could see the glee in her eyes! She

had archived what she had came here for. To plunge me into the

madness and steal my man!! I began to cry. I could feel the

madness taking control of me. Camaz picked me up and cradled

me to his chest and shot straight up into the air and flew me back

to the castle. By the time we reached home I was already losing

it! I was seeing horrible creatures everywhere! He tried to

reassure me there was nothing there. But I was out of my head

with fear. I was screaming and telling him to get them away from

me. He had taken me the healers to see if they can do anything for

me. They told him it was very rare for a vampire comes out after

being bitten by a ghoul. That only I could release myself from the

madness. Through all of my madness I was listening to what the healers were telling Camaz. I withdrew into my mind along with all of the monsters that came with me. I was in constant battle with them! But I would continue to fight until I ether died or was released from the madness and if I made it, Katrina was going to pay with her life!!

Chapter 55

THE MADNESS

I didn't know how long I had been fighting the madness or if I
was winning, but all I did know was the hatred was building
within me! That was helping me fight the madness. I was
defeating more and more of the monsters with each day. I could
hear Camaz talking to me, telling me how much he loved me
and he would wait all of eternity for my return. He was in my
mind with me and his soothing voice was helping me to
concentrate. I was in battle with the worst monster I had ever seen
but I could see no others anymore. I had to defeat that beast to
escape the madness. He was huge, with glowing red skin, horns
atop his head and a long pointed tail. His mouth was full of razor
sharp teeth. I thought to myself, "My god, I am fighting the devil
himself! He wants my soul and will stop at nothing to get it!"
He then spoke, "Come on little vampire, give in, you know you

cannot defeat me!" I was really pissed, he had used the two words

I hated the most! I felt the fire building within me. I drew my

sword and said, "Okay devil, let's dance!" I then rushed at him

full force. I jumped into the air and came down swinging. I caught

him across his chest and he screamed out in pain. I was back up

on my feet and we began our dance of death. I screamed out in

my mind to Camaz, "I love you." and I took on the beast. I could

hear Camaz in my mind saying, "Fight fierce, my warrior queen

and come back to me!" The beast and I began to circle each other.

He roared and rushed me. I sidestepped him and swung my

sword. I caught him in the neck. My blade cut deep but it did not

remove his head. He was furious, he swung around and raked his

huge claws down my chest. I screamed out in pain, but I had no

time to stop, he was coming for me again. I leaped up into the air

and landed on the beast's back. I removed my daggers and

slammed them into his neck. He fell backwards onto me. I rolled

as soon as I hit the ground and I was on top of him. I raised my sword and with one final blow removed his head. At that moment I opened my eyes and stared into the face of an angel! My beloved Camaz! I looked around the room but he was the only one present. With trembling lips I said, "Is it over? Or have I died and gone to heaven?" He bent down and kissed my cheek and said, "My one true love, it is over and you have fought your way back to me through the madness!" I began to cry and with the blood tears flowing down my cheeks I said, "Oh baby, I thought I would never get back to you! I even fought the devil himself to get back to you!" He wiped the tears from my cheeks and said, "If I could have fought the beasts for you, I would have taken them all on and would have given up my life for you gladly!" I reached for him and pulled him down to my lips kissing him madly. But I broke our kiss and asked, "Where is Katrina? Is she still here?" "Yes my love she is still here, why do you ask?" I looked him directly in the eye and said, "Bring her to me!!" Camaz told me she was heavy with Samuel and Kim's child and couldn't leave

her quarters. He asked, "Why do you need to see her my queen?"
I looked up at him again and started to cry, but this time they were
tears of anger! I said, "Because she is the one that arraigned for us
to be attacked by the ghouls and for me being bitten!" I proceeded
to tell him what I had observed during the battle and how her
fight with the ghoul was staged. He looked at me with anger in his
eyes and said, "If this is true my queen, then I shall kill her
myself!" I told him, "Oh no, that pleasure will be all mine! That is
what keep me fighting the madness. The thought of making her
pay for what she had done to me!" "Very well my dear, but she
will not be dealt with until after the child is born." He would later
tell me she would stand before the council for her crimes and if
judged guilty it would be my right to kill her. I thought, "Oh
goodie, I can hardly wait! I would stay away from her until the
child was born, but then she will be mine!" A few weeks later she
gave birth to a son. He was taken from her at once and she was
taken down below and locked in a cell to await her trial. She

asked, "Why are you doing this to me? I have done nothing to deserve this treatment!" At that point I walked up to her cell and she gasped. I could see the fear building in her eyes. I answered, "you know exactly what you have done and now you will pay for it with your life!" At that point she screamed at me, " He loves me! He has loved me since the day of our union. You are nothing to him!" I laughed and said, "I know better bitch, Camaz is my soul mate and one true love, as I am to him. You would have never been able to be with him, even if the madness had won and killed me! Enjoy your time down here. I will see you in a few days at the trial." I left the room laughing all the way out. A few days later she stood before our council for her crimes. A ghoul from the tribe that attacked us had been captured and he told the story of her whole plot to have his life spared. The council proclaimed judgment on her of death by my hands. I had decided to engage her in hand to hand combat. I was going to have so much fun ripping her to pieces! The night before her execution I laid in bed with Camaz talking. He told me he was furious with

Katrina and he didn't even like being with her when Mikel was

conceived. He told me again that I was his one true love and there

could be no other. He made love to me that night like no other. I

fell asleep with a smile on my face. The next evening when I

arose I dressed for battle. The only thing I did not bring with me

were my weapons. I had chosen to kill her with my bare hands. A

few minutes later we were standing in the battle area where many

vampires had trained, including myself. She was on one side of

the area, I on the other. I yelled to her, "Okay bitch, are you ready

for me?" I knew she was a royal and many years older than me

but she had been pampered her whole life and was weak. I ran at

her and knocked her to the ground. I was on her in a flash,

straddling her chest. I looked down at her and smiled I then

proceed to rip her throat out. I stood and watched the life leave

her body. I smiled to myself, went to Camaz, and took his hand

saying, "Let's go home!" The madness had taken quite a toll on me, so for now I am going to end my stories. But I will pick up

my pen in the near future and tell you more of my wonderful life.

Made in the USA
Charleston, SC
25 February 2016